Anonymous

Quaker Strongholds

Anonymous

Quaker Strongholds

ISBN/EAN: 9783337395575

Printed in Europe, USA, Canada, Australia, Japan

Cover: Foto ©Andreas Hilbeck / pixelio.de

More available books at **www.hansebooks.com**

QUAKER STRONGHOLDS

BY

CAROLINE EMELIA STEPHEN

AUTHOR OF "THE SERVICE OF THE POOR."

THIRD EDITION

LONDON

EDWARD HICKS, JUN., 14, BISHOPSGATE WITHOUT.

1891.

PREFACE TO THE THIRD EDITION.

Of the comments which have been made on this book, there is but one to which I wish to make any reply. Some of my readers have regretted the absence from its pages of any reference to certain fundamental doctrines of Christianity : and have, I fear, more or less misunderstood my silence in this direction.

It is true that I have contented myself with trying to explain what is, for practical purposes, the strength of our special position as compared with that of our fellow-disciples—wherein consist the strongholds of that separate testimony which we desire to maintain in its purity.

This attempt did not, in my view, involve any need for a full exposition of our Christian faith—that faith "once delivered to the saints" which we hold in common with the whole Christian Church. Friends have never professed any separate theological or historical creed : and it did not occur to me that the strict limitation of my subject to matters of practice and of spiritual experience could give rise to any doubts of the breadth and fulness of our unity with our fellow-Christians as to the common root and source of all our faith and hope.

There is, however, no doubt something distinctive in our theology, as well as in our practice, for the two things cannot be wholly separated. So far as I know, the main points of doctrine upon which the early Friends were accustomed to find themselves in opposition to the prevailing thought of their day, lay in their boldly-proclaimed belief in "the universality of the saving light of Christ," and in the possibility of being even in this life so made free from sin as to "stand perfect in our present rank." They were accustomed not only to admit, but to insist, that the heathen, who had not the outward knowledge of Christ, were saved by His power, light, and grace without such outward knowledge if they were but faithful to the light they had°—"willing and obedient" in submitting to the Divine visitations extended, in some measure, to every child of man. And at the same time they indignantly rejected as a "pleading for imperfection" the common notion that not even the fullest acceptance of the Gospel in its purity could bring any of us into entire freedom from sin in this life. In regard to all conditions of men they boldly used the language of unhesitating confidence in the justice and the mercy of God, who would reward every man according to his works.†

I will not venture to say that all those who now bear the name of Friends are still faithful to this testimony. The questions most frequently and eagerly discussed in these days are not the same as those on which, 200 years

---

° See Wm. Penn's "No Cross, No Crown."—passim.

† See Barclay's Apology, Props. V., VI., and VIII.

ago, Friends fought their hardest controversial battles. I scarcely know whether such doctrines as I have just referred to would or would not now be considered as altogether "orthodox" outside the Society; but I am sure that while human hearts are alive to the eternal welfare of their brethren, that religion must seem the most Divine, which has in it the least of what is merely arbitrary—which relies least for spiritual safety upon an outward knowledge shared only by the few; and that that view of Divine justice will ever be felt as least unworthy which most stedfastly refuses to believe in the possibility of God's requiring from all that which He has not put within the power of all.

Both the beliefs in question seem indeed to flow naturally from a deep personal experience of Divine light as a constant and all-penetrating influence, in the midst of which we live and move and have our being. A revelation reaching to the inmost depths of even one human heart must inevitably embrace also the widest range of human needs. The light of the very Sun of Righteousness cannot be other than central and all-pervading. Men may (and do) shut their eyes to it, as to the outward daylight; or whilst obeying it they may fail to recognise its nature and source; but it is not possible to recognise it as Divine and yet to think of it as less universal in its range than the outward sunshine which is bestowed by the Father of all upon the just and the unjust.

It is not, however, so much in the contents of our theology as in our attitude towards theology that there

A

is a distinctive element, and it is in reference to this characteristic attitude of the Quaker mind, and my own share in it, that I desire especially to make my meaning clear.

It is well known that Friends have always abstained on principle from the use of creeds and formularies, either as parts of worship or as a condition of membership; although they have never been slow to vindicate their faith, whether in its distinctive or in its broadly Christian aspects. This task has indeed been so abundantly performed both by individual Friends and by the Yearly Meetings in their collective utterances * that it would have been doubly unwise for me to

———

* The volume to which I have repeatedly referred by its present title of "The Book of Discipline" (formerly known as "The Book of Extracts"), is the latest of a series of similar volumes of Extracts from the proceedings of London Yearly Meeting, issued and revised from time to time by its authority. And to these volumes I must refer those who desire to see the fullest exposition of the theological views of the Society. The successive editions bear the following dates:—1783, 1802, 1834, a supplement in 1849, 1861, and 1883. At each of these revisions some change has been made in the passages selected for quotation: and the change in the proportional space assigned in them to various aspects of the truth must, I suppose, be held to reflect with more or less accuracy the changes which have gradually taken place in the prevailing tone of thought in the Society. I am quite unable to attempt even an outline of these changes, and indeed, interesting as a study of them might be to the curious in such matters, I cannot feel that it would in any degree help forward my one object of making clear the ideal to which Friends, as such, are specially pledged.

attempt a task for which I am not qualified. I have entire unity with that caution in speaking of Divine things which is so deeply ingrained a characteristic of the Quaker mind. The practice of silence as an essential preparation for any edifying approach to the utmost sanctuary no doubt largely influences all our habits of thought and speech. We do not much seek to surround our beliefs with precise verbal outlines. With a wise simplicity, in which I desire to share, Friends have said* that in speaking of the working of Redeeming Love "we prefer the use of such terms as we find in Scripture ; and contented with that knowledge which Divine wisdom hath seen meet to reveal, we attempt not to explain those mysteries which remain under the veil." We have ever trusted to the influence of the Divine Spirit, rather than to any form of words, for guidance into all truth.

A deep-rooted trust in the all penetrating power of Divine Light, also naturally tends in some degree to check that impatience to "teach every man his neighbour," which is intelligible enough in those who regard human teaching as the only means whereby a knowledge supposed to be necessary to salvation can be diffused. The immediate result of the reception of light in one's own heart is indeed the impulse to communicate it by bearing witness to it —to kindle (so far as heart can kindle heart)—an answering flame in others—and thus,

---

* Summary of the History, Doctrine and Discipline of Friends, published by the authority of the Meeting for Sufferings, in or about 1790.

as by beacon fires, to spread from height to height the glad tidings of salvation. But not always, nor chiefly, by words is this kindling process effected. Words may and do fail again and again in the thick of the "good fight." The very intensity of the fire of faith tends, I believe, to fuse doctrine into entreaty, and words into influence. Anxiety about the precise statement of truth at any rate is apt to be consumed by a fervent desire for the prevalence of obedience to truth.

It is, perhaps, not surprising that our habitual abstinence from the attempt to define the undefinable and to formulate for transmission to others those mysteries before which the deepest human wisdom most deeply feels its own insufficiency, should have been much and often misunderstood. It has led to many doubts of our orthodoxy as a body ; and, coupled with our disuse of outward ordinances, it has led some even to question our Christianity.

It is here that any misinterpretation of our silence naturally touches us to the quick. Doubts of each other's "orthodoxy" have been so freely interchanged in all directions amongst Christians as to have lost much of their force. But no true Christian will contentedly acquiesce in any doubt as to his loyalty to Christ. And silence may of course proceed from the most various sources—from unbelief and from indifference, as well as from reverence and from adoration. I desire, therefore, on my own behalf, as well as on behalf of those with whom I have any true religious fellowship, to say in the most emphatic manner that the liberty we claim—and proclaim—from forms and formularies is not the liberty to think our own thoughts and to go our own way. It is, on the contrary, the liberty wherewith Christ Himself hath made us free—the liberty of those who, having the substance, know that they no longer need the figure—the liberty which comes of taking up our cross and following Him who was crucified for us.

Our objection to forms is not that they would pledge us too deeply, but rather that they would confine us to that which is too little—that they hamper and check the living exercise of the spirit which is necessary for real worship and real inward growth. Quakerism, as I understand it, is largely a protest against the attempt to reduce spiritual life to a technical process—a matter of rules and definitions to be confidently applied and transmitted by human agents, and separable from the growth of the Divine seed in the heart. We feel this growth to be mainly beyond human ken—a hidden birth proceeding from a source unfathomable by the human mind.

And if this be true of that part of the "mystery of godliness" which relates to our own life and experience—if even in regard to what takes place in our own hearts we feel a sacred fear of inter-meddling in the mysterious processes of life and growth by intellectual investigation or effort of will—how much more must we fear to give free play to words, or even to thoughts, respecting the nature of the very Fountain from which our eternal life is derived ; and the awful and mysterious manner in which alone, under necessities for ever inscrutable by us, that Fountain could be opened to us?

To know in our own experience that eternal life is indeed freely opened to us—that it is possible for us to be redeemed and healed and made one in Christ, as He is one with the Father—to know that for our sakes the Son of God did lay down His life, becoming obedient unto death, even the death upon the cross, that we, through Him, might have life—to know in our own hearts what it is to be brought under the humbling, redeeming, purifying power of the cross of Christ—all this is enough and more than enough to fill our lips with praise and our hearts with thanksgiving, and to set us free for ever from the desire for explanations of the unspeakable. As through death life is opened to us, so—whether slowly or suddenly, yet surely, as in a heavenly dawn—does the "Radiancy Divine," the "brightness of the Father's glory," become visible to us, and we recognize it for what it is—"the light of the knowledge of the glory of God, in the face of Jesus Christ." Why this revelation must be through death —why we could be redeemed only through His submission for our sakes to "endure the shame," to drink the bitterest cup ever tasted on this earth, to suffer the extremest penalty of the sin He never shared—this we may indeed partly feel, but no tongue can tell.

If therefore we do not always utter freely, or confidently define, our belief as to the nature and work of our Lord Jesus Christ, it is not for want of absolute and adoring trust in Him as the Lamb of God that taketh away the sins of the world; but because the mystery is greater and the trust deeper—fuller, broader, more powerful—than words can utter: because we dare not limit or define in terms of the intellect that which can be understood only by the child-like heart; because as we "look upon Him whom we have pierced," but Who yet has loved us with an everlasting love, and given Himself for us, that the love of the Father to us sinners might be livingly revealed to us—as we look upon Him, the only language possible to us is the language of penitence, of praise, of love, and of adoration.

C. E. S.

Mount Pleasant,
    West Malvern, 1890.

CONTENTS.

QUAKER STRONGHOLDS.

—:

INTRODUCTION.

WHETHER Quakerism be, as some Friends believe, destined to any considerable revival or not, it seems at least certain that any important revival of religion must be the result of a fresh recognition and acceptance of the very principles upon which the Society of Friends is built. What these principles and the practices resulting from them really are, is a subject on which there is a surprising amount of ignorance amongst us, considering how widely spread is the connection with and interest about Friends amongst the members of other persuasions. One seldom meets any one who has not some link with the Society, and yet it is rare to find any one not belonging to it at all accurately informed as to its point of view or its organization. The notorious disinclination of Friends to any attempts at proselytizing, and perhaps some lingering effects of persecution, probably account for the very common impression that Friends' meetings are essentially private—mysterious gatherings into which it would be intrusive to seek admission. Many people, indeed, probably suppose (if they think about it at all) that such meetings are no longer held ; that the Society is fast dying out, and the "silent worship" of tradition a thing of the past—impracticable, and hardly to be seriously mentioned in these days of talk and of breathless activity.

Some such vague impression floated, I believe, over my own mind, when, some seventeen years ago, I first found myself within reach of a Friends' meeting, and. somewhat to my surprise, was cordially made welcome to attend it. The invitation came at a moment of need, for I was beginning to feel with dismay that I might not much longer be able conscientiously to continue to join in the Church of England service : not for want of appreciation of its unrivalled richness and beauty, but from doubts of the truth of its doctrines, combined with a growing recognition that to me it was as the armour of Saul in its elaboration and in the sustained pitch of religious fervour for which it was meant to provide an utterance. Whether true or not in its speculative and theoretical assumptions, it was clear to me that it was far from true as a periodical expression of my own experience, belief, or aspiration. The more vividly one feels the force of its eloquence, the more, it seems to me, one must hesitate to adopt it as the language of one's own soul, and the more unlikely is it that such heights and depths of feeling as it demands should be ready to fill its magnificent channels every Sunday morning at a given hour. The questionings with which at that period I was painfully struggling were stirred into redoubled activity by the dogmatic statements and assumptions with which the Liturgy

abounds, and its unbroken flow left no loophole for the
utterance of my own less disciplined, but to myself far
more urgent, cries for help.   Thus the hour of public
worship, which should have been a time of spiritual
strengthening and calming, became to me a time of
renewed conflict, and of occasional exaltation and excitement of emotion, leading but too surely to reaction
and apathy.

I do not attempt to pass any judgment on this
mental condition.   I have described it at some length
because I cannot believe it to be altogether exceptional,
or without significance. At any rate, it was fast leading
me to dread the moment when I should be unable either
to find the help I needed, or to offer my tribute of
devotion, in any place of worship amongst my fellow-
Christians.   When lo, on one never-to-be-forgotten
Sunday morning, I found myself one of a small
company of silent worshippers, who were content to sit
down together without words, that each one might
feel after and draw near to the Divine Presence, un-
hindered at least, if not helped, by any human utterance.
Utterance I knew was free, should the words be given :
and before the meeting was over, a sentence or two
were uttered in great simplicity by an old and apparently
untaught man, rising in his place amongst the rest of
us. I did not pay much attention to the words he spoke,
and I have no recollection of their purport.   My whole
soul was filled with the unutterable peace of the undisturbed opportunity for communion with God—with
the sense that at last I had found a place where I
might, without the faintest suspicion of insincerity,

join with others in simply seeking His presence. To sit down in silence could at the least pledge me to nothing ; it might open to me (as it did that morning) the very gate of heaven. And since that day, now more than seventeen years ago, Friends' meetings have indeed been to me the greatest of outward helps to a fuller and fuller entrance into the spirit from which they have sprung : the place of the most soul-subduing, faith-restoring, strengthening and peaceful communion, in feeding upon the bread of life, that I have ever known. I cannot but believe that what has helped me so un-speakably might be helpful to multitudes in this day of shaking of all that can be shaken, and of restless inquiry after spiritual good. It is in the hope of making more widely known the true source and nature of such spiritual help that I am about to attempt to describe what I have called our strongholds—those principles which cannot fail, whatever may be the future of the Society which for more than two hundred years has taken its stand upon them. I wish to trace, as far as my experience as a "convinced Friend" enables me to do so, what is the true life and strength of our Society ; and the manner in which its principles, as actually embodied in its practice, its organization, and above all, its manner of worship, are fitted to meet the special needs of an important class in our own day.

CHAPTER I.

ORGANIZATION.

THE actual organization of the Society of Friends is, I believe, by no means familiarly known outside its own borders, and a slight sketch of it may be neither uninteresting in itself, nor out of place as a preliminary to the endeavour to explain our general position. I propose, therefore, to give such an outline of our constitution as a Society, so far as I have become acquainted with it. The fullest details respecting it are to be found in the "Book of Discipline," which is the authorized exponent of all such matters.

This book has been recently revised, and the edition of 1883* (a large octavo volume) contains the latest regulations on all points of internal government. The Yearly Meeting also publishes annually a volume of Extracts from its proceedings, a full statement of

---

* "Book of Christian Discipline of the Religious Society of Friends in Great Britain : consisting of Extracts on Doctrine, Practice, and Church Government, from the Epistles and other Documents issued under the sanction of the Yearly Meeting held in London from its first institution in 1672 to 1883." London : Samuel Harris and Co., 5, Bishopsgate Street Without. 1883.

accounts and statistics, and a summary of the reports received from the subordinate meetings all over the country.

Every "particular meeting," that is, every congregation meeting habitually for worship on the first (and generally also on one other) day of the week, is one of a group of meetings for worship (usually about five or six) which meet together once a month, for the transaction of business and of discipline, and which together form what is therefore called a Monthly Meeting. Each Monthly Meeting, again, is one of a group of probably four or five Monthly Meetings, which in like manner unite to form a Quarterly Meeting, at whose quarterly sittings matters of larger importance are considered ; and the eighteen Quarterly Meetings of Great Britian form in their turn the London Yearly Meeting, which is the supreme authority in the Society. It may in a certain sense be said indeed, that it *is* the Society of Friends of Great Britian, for every Friend is a member of the Monthly, Quarterly, and Yearly Meetings to which he or she belongs, and is entitled to a voice in all their deliberations. The Yearly Meeting assembles in May, and its sittings, which are held, as they have been from the first, in Devonshire House, Bishopsgate Street, last generally about a fortnight. The actual attendance, is, of course, small in comparison with the number of members. At the present time the Society in Great Britain consists of about fifteen thousand members, and the annual gatherings in Bishopsgate Street number perhaps from twelve to fifteen hundred.

The men and women sit separately, or rather to speak quite correctly the men and women Friends have each a separate Yearly Meeting; the Women's Yearly Meeting being of considerably later date than the men's. It was established in 1790, and it deals in general with matters of less importance, or at any rate of more restricted scope, than the men's meeting. It is, however, not unusual for men Friends, " under religious concern," to visit the women's meeting, nor for women Friends on a similar ground to visit that of the men.

"Joint sittings "—meetings, that is, of men and women Friends in one body—are also held occasionally, when any question of special interest to all the members is to be considered, and on these occasions the women are free to take their full share in the discussions. These occasional combinations are the more easily practicable, because, strange as it may seem to most people, no question is ever put to the vote. From the earliest times, all decisions have been arrived at by what may be called a practical unanimity. The Yearly Meeting, like every other meeting for " business " or " discipline," has its clerk, who, with one or more assistants, performs the combined functions of chairman and secretary. When any question has been fully considered, it is the duty of the clerk to interpret the sense of the meeting, and to prepare a minute accordingly; which minute, being read to the meeting, often receives a certain amount of verbal, or even of substantial modification, in accordance with the suggestions of individual Friends; but, when entered upon the books, is accepted as embodying the decision of the meeting. Should there be any considerable division of judgment upon any important question, it is usually, if possible, adjourned till the next Yearly Meeting : and this plan has, I believe, been almost invariably found sufficient to bring about the practical unanimity required for a final settlement of the question. It is certainly a very remarkable fact that so large a body should transact all its affairs without ever voting, to the full satisfaction of the great majority of those concerned.

The Quarterly and Monthly Meetings are, in most respects, repetitions on a smaller scale of the Yearly Meeting. The business of all these subordinate meetings is transacted, like that of the Yearly Meeting, without voting, and settled similarly through the action of the clerk when a practical unanimity is arrived at. Each Monthly Meeting appoints "representatives" to the next Quarterly Meeting, and the Quarterly Meetings, in like manner appoint "representatives" to the Yearly Meeting. These Friends have no very definite function to perform, but their names are called over, and their presence or absence noted at the opening of each meeting to which they are sent : and they are expected to serve in a general way as a special medium of communication between the larger and the smaller meetings to which they belong.

In like manner, upon any subject affecting the Society at large, the Yearly Meeting communicates with the Quarterly Meetings, who in their turn diffuse the impulse through their own Monthly and particular meetings, till it reaches every individual member ;

and, in return, information respecting every meeting for worship is from time to time given to the Monthly Meetings, to be by them in a condensed form reported to the Quarterly Meetings, and so eventually presented to the Yearly Meeting in London. All these ascending and descending processes are carried on with minute accuracy and regularity, and are duly recorded at every stage in the books of each meeting. There is thus a complete system of circulation, as of veins and arteries, by which every individual member is brought within reach of the Society at large, and through which information, influence, and discipline are carried to and from the centre and the extremities.

The "discipline" of the Society is a matter of extreme interest, as to which I cannot venture to say with any confidence how far our recognised ideal is actually carried out in practice. There is no doubt that of late years considerable changes have taken place, mainly in the direction of a relaxation of discipline with regard to comparatively trivial matters. Certain "queries" have from the earliest times been appointed by the authority of the Yearly Meeting, to be read and considered at certain seasons in the subordinate meetings, and to most of these queries (some relating to various branches of Christian morality, and some to regularity in attendance at meetings and conformity to established standards of simplicity in dress and language) it was formerly the practice to require detailed answers from each particular meeting, to be in due course transmitted in a summarized form to the Yearly Meeting itself. In 1861, however, the Yearly Meeting issued directions that a certain number of these queries should be merely " considered," but not answered. In 1875 this method was adopted with regard to nearly all the queries, and at present those only which relate to the regularity of attendance at meetings for worship and business are answered.* This change has a very obvious significance, and I believe that its effect is even more marked than would be understood by any one not accustomed to the extreme care and gravity with which these matters were formerly pondered and reported upon in each, " preparative meeting " (*i.e.* each particular meeting sitting specially with a view to preparing the business to be transacted at any approaching Monthly Meeting), and again at each stage of the progress of the report towards its final presentation by the Quarterly to the Yearly Meeting. Dress and language and other external matters are now practically left entirely to the individual conscience, as is surely wisest. With regard to weightier matters, such as strict integrity in business, sobriety, and correctness of moral conduct, etc., there is still, I hope and believe, a considerable reality of watchful care exercised through specially appointed members. In every Monthly Meeting there are Friends holding the offices of elder and overseer. The business of the elders is to watch over the ministers in the exercise of their gift ; that of the overseers to see to the relief of the poorer members, the care of the sick, and other such matters : to watch over the

---

* The queries now in use are given at length in the Appendix, Note A.

members generally with regard to their Christian conduct, to warn privately any who may be giving cause of offence or scandal, and in case of need to bring the matter before the Monthly Meeting to be dealt with as it may require. Should the Monthly Meeting think it necessary to disown a member for persisting in conduct not consistent with our Christian profession, or for any other reason, the member in question may appeal to the Quarterly Meeting, and from its decision to that of the Yearly Meeting, which is in all cases final.

The London Yearly Meeting has two standing committees for the transaction of such of its affairs as need attention more frequently than once a year. One of these represents the Yearly Meeting at large, and has charge of its money matters and other general business; it bears the curious and suggestive title of the "Meeting for Sufferings," from having been originally occupied mainly in relieving Friends under Persecution. The other is a committee of the Yearly Meeting on Ministry and Oversight, and is called the "Morning Meeting."

Meetings on Ministry and Oversight are held in every Quarterly and Monthly Meeting as well as at the Yearly Meeting. They are composed of all the recorded ministers, the elders and overseers of each meeting, together with (in some Quarterly Meetings) some Friends described as "associate members," who attend them as it were not officially, but by a standing invitation. These meetings are concerned, of course, with questions relating to the special offices exercised by their members.

The ministers are, as is well known, not appointed or set apart by any human ordination, nor are any of them ever paid, or liable to be called upon by any human authority, for any ministerial services. By the word " ministers " we mean simply those, be they men or women, who have received a gift and call to minister, that is to offer vocal service, in meetings for worship. When any Friend has exercised such a gift for a considerable time in a manner which is recognised by the other members as evincing a true vocation, the Monthly Meeting proceeds to record the fact on the books of the meeting. This acknowledgment is made merely for the sake of " good order," and is not supposed to confer any additional power or authority on the minister " recorded." The ministers are perfectly free to continue their ordinary occupations, and many of them are, in fact, engaged in earning their own living in trades, business, or professions.

When a minister, in the exercises of his or her gift, feels called to travel to any distant place, it is thought right that the " concern " should be laid before the Monthly Meeting, and, should it be an important or distant concern, before the Quarterly and, in some cases, even the Yearly Meeting also ; when the meetings in question will, if they feel " unity " with it, give the minister a minute or certificate to that effect, which serves as an introduction and guarantee in whatever meetings the minister may visit during that " service." In such cases the ministers' travelling expenses are paid from one Monthly or Quarterly Meeting to another, and it is usual for them to be welcomed into the houses

of some of the Friends belonging to the meetings
visited. The extent to which Friends do thus travel,
both in England and abroad, " in the service of Truth,"
is something of which few people outside the Society
have any idea. Between England and America there
is a continual interchange of such visits, and the very
copious biographical literature of the Society teems
with the records of journeys undertaken " under an
impression of religious duty," and lasting sometimes
for months, or even years, before the Friend could " feel
clear " of the work. No limit is ever set beforehand
to such work. It is felt to be work in which the daily
unfolding of the Divine ordering must be watched and
waited for.

Such is a general outline of what may be called the
machinery of the Society. It remains to state briefly
its distinguishing tenets before preceeding to consider
the spirit and inner spring from which these outward
developments have arisen, and from whence they derive
all their significance and value.

I have already referred to the peculiarity which lies
at the root of all the rest : namely, our views as to the
nature of the true gospel ministry, as a call bestowed
on men and women, on old or young, learned and
unlearned : bestowed directly from above and not to
be conferred by any human authority, or hired for
money : to be exercised under the sole and immediate
direction of the one master, the only Head of the
Church, Christ the Lord. As a consequence of this
view, Friends have, as is well known, refused as a
matter of conscience to pay tithes, or in any way to

contribute to the maintenance of a paid ministry, and of the services prescribed by the Established Church.

Closely connected with these views on ministry is our testimony against the observance of any religious rites or ceremonies whatever. Neither baptizing with water, nor the breaking of bread and drinking of wine, are recognized by us as Divinely ordained institutions of permanent obligation, and neither of these ceremonies is practised by us. We believe that the coming of Christ put an end to the old dispensation of outward observances, and that the whole drift of His teaching was against the attaching of importance to such things. The passages relating to His last supper with His disciples, and those in which He speaks of His permanent influence upon them under the images of bread, blood, etc., seem to us much more intelligible and impressive when understood without reference to the sacramental theories which have been engrafted upon them. The one baptism " with the Holy Ghost and with fire," and the continual spiritual communion to be enjoyed in feeding on the bread of life, are felt by us to be of the very essence of true and spiritual worship ; but we believe them to be entirely independent of any outward observances. We therefore feel that no other condition is needed for the highest acts of worship than the presence, and the right spiritual disposition, of the worshippers.

The rejection of any separate priesthood, and of all outward observances, is the main divergence between us and other Christians. We have always maintained a testimony against war as inconsistent with the full acceptance of the Spirit of Christ, and against oaths as distinctly forbidden by Him.   We have also been led to abandon the pursuit of changing fashions, and to cherish a plainness in dress and language of a marked character, now fast changing its type, but not, we trust, really disappearing.   These minor testimonies are probably more widely known than the more fundamental ones ; and, though concerned with comparatively trivial matters, they also spring from a deep oot of principle.   It is a remarkable fact that from time to time religious bodies have sprung up in various parts of the world, who, without any communication with us, have adopted similar views on many, if not all, of these points.   This fact, as well as the continuance and the widely spread influence of our own Society, seems to show that its roots lie deep in some fundamental principles of truth.

I am now about to attempt to deal with those principles, not in the way of analysis or with any attempt at precision of language, but as a record of their practical working, gathered mainly from personal experience.   It is not, I confess, without some anxiety that I, as a new-comer, enter upon this task. In the preceding sketch of matters of fact, it has of course been easy to guard against any serious misstatements : but in the following chapters I must deal with matters less easily verifiable.   It seems to me in some respects hardly possible that any one not born and bred in the Society should be fully qualified to unfold its principles and practices.   There is, on the other hand, in the very act of having entered it from with-

out, a special qualification for the office of interpreting
them to outsiders. It will, I hope, be remembered
that I have no kind of claim to speak in any sense in
the name of the Society. My object is to explain (so
so far as the experience of ten years' membership may
enable me) the secret of its strength and its attraction
for others ; and for this attempt one brought up outside
its pale, and speaking in a purely individual capacity,
may well feel a special freedom. If I cannot pretend
to possess the entirely correct accent of a born Friend,
I may be none the less intelligible to those amongst
whom my own Christian principles were imbibed and
nourished until the years of maturity.

CHAPTER II.

THE INNER LIGHT.

THE one corner stone of belief upon which the Society of Friends is built is the conviction that God does indeed communicate with each one of the spirits He has made, in a direct and living inbreathing of some measure of the breath of His own Life; that He never leaves Himself without a witness in the heart as well as in the surroundings of man; that the measure of light, life, or grace thus given increases by obedience; and that in order clearly to hear the Divine voice speaking within us we need to be still: to be alone with Him, in the secret place of His Presence: that all flesh should keep silence before Him.

This belief may be more precisely stated, explained and as we think justified, by those who are competent to deal with it in a philosophical manner. The founders of our Society were not philosophers, but spoke of these things from an intense and abundant personal experience, which led them with confidence to appeal to the experience of all sorts and conditions of men for confirmation of their doctrine as to the light within. And they were not disappointed. The history of the sudden gathering of the Society, of its rapid formation into a strongly organized body, and of the extraordinary constancy, zeal, and integrity displayed by its original members, is a most impressive proof of the trueness of their aim.*

I have no ambition to clothe the fundamental doctrine of our Society in any less popular language than that in which it was originally preached. I would rather, even did necessity not compel me, be content to appeal, as did the early Friends, to common experience. My aim is to explain for practical purposes, and in modern as well as simple language, the way in which our whole constitution as a Society, and our various special testimonies, have resulted from this one main principle.

When questioned as to the reality and nature of the light within, the early Friends were accustomed in return to ask the questioners whether they did not sometimes feel something within them that showed them their sins ; and to assure them that this same power, which *made manifest*, and therefore was truly light, would also, if yielded to, lead them out of sin. This assurance, that the light which revealed was also the power which would heal sin, was George Fox's gospel. The power itself was described by him in many ways.

---

* It is estimated that in 1680 (or thirty-two years from the beginning of George Fox's ministry) the number of Friends was about 40,000. "In 1656 Fox computed that there were seldom less than 1,000 in prison ; and it has been asserted that, between 1661 and 1697, 13,562 Quakers were imprisoned, 152 were transported, and 338 died in prison or of their wounds " (" Encycl. Brit.," 9th edit., art. " Quakers ").

Christ within, the hope of glory ; the light, life, Spirit, and grace of Christ ; the seed, the new birth, the power of God unto salvation, and many other such expressions, flow forth in abundant streams of heartfelt eloquence. To "turn people to the light within," to "direct them to Christ, their free Teacher," was his daily business.

For this purpose he and his friends travelled continually up and down the country, holding meetings everywhere, and finding a never-failing response to their appeal, as is proved by the bare numbers of those who, within a very few years, were ready to encounter persecution, and to maintain their testimony through long years of imprisonment and sufferings. In the earlier days of the Society the doctrine of the light within was clearly one readily understood and accepted by the ordinary English mind. In our own day it is usually spoken of as a mysterious tenet, springing up now and again in the minds of isolated enthusiasts, but indigenous only in Oriental countries, and naturally abhorrent to the practical common sense of our own people.

The difference arises, I think, from the fact that there are circles within circles, or spheres within spheres, and that the light to which the early Friends bore witness was not *confined* to that innermost sanctuary of whose very existence, perhaps, none but a few "mystics" are conscious ; but that, while proceeding from those deepest depths, it was recognised as also lighting up conscience, and conduct, and all the tangible outer framework of life ; and that it was called "within" not alone in the sense of lying nearer

the centre of our being than anything else, but also in
the (to ordinary minds) more intelligible sense of
beginning at home—of being the reward of each man's
own faithfulness, of being independent of priests and
ordinances. The religion they preached was one which
enforced the individual responsibility of each one for
his own soul : it was a portable and verifiable religion—
a religion which required truth in word and deed, plain
dealing and kindness and self-control, and which did
not require ceremonial observances or priestly guaran-
tees : a religion in which practice went for more than
theory, and all were expected to take their stand on one
level, and their share in the worship and the business
of "the church." It is easy to see how such preaching
as this would commend itself to English independence.
It surely commends itself to the unchanging sense of
truth in the human heart, and will be welcomed
whenever it is preached from first-hand experience of
its power.

"That which you seek without you have already
within you." The words which changed the life of
Madame Guyon will never lose their power while
human nature is occupied with the struggle for a state
of stable equilibrium. The perennial justification of
Quakerism lies in its energetic assertion that the kingdom
of heaven is within us ; that we are not made dependent
upon any outward organization for our spiritual
welfare. Its perennial difficulty lies in the inveterate
disposition of human beings to look to each other for
spiritual help, in the feebleness of their perception
of that Divine Voice which speaks to each one in a

language no other ear can hear, and in the apathy which is content to go through life without the attempt at any true individual communion with God.

"The kingdom of heaven is within us." No Christian disputes the truth of this deep word of Christ Himself. But its interpretation has a wide range. In His own lips it was used in opposition to the "Lo here! and lo there!" for which he was preparing His Disciples. They were not to be hurried away into a search for Christ in all directions, but were to remember that His kingdom (surely implying His living presence) is in the hearts of His people. He Himself makes none of those abstruse distinctions between consciousness and being, accident and essence, subject and object, or even superficial and profound, and so forth, which it has been the delight of many of His most devoted followers to interweave with this simple expression "within you."

I think it is inevitable that the more deeply we penetrate into the recesses of the human mind, the more we should have a sense of approaching an inner sanctuary, and that there is a very real and deep sense in which this word "within you" may be understood as meaning "above all in your inmost depths." But this is not its original or its obvious meaning. In the teaching of our Lord there is a frequent reference to the distinction of inward and outward, but the distinction is drawn in a broad and simple manner. It is oftenest a demand upon our sincerity and thoroughness, not upon our powers of introspection—an appeal on behalf of the weightier matters of the Law as compared with trivial and ceremonial observances. It would scarcely, I think, be true to say that the doctrine of an "inward light," as we understand it, is explicitly laid down in the Gospels, although, to my own mind, that doctrine appears to be an almost inevitable inference from their teaching. I am not, however, attempting to deal with the question on its merits. I only wish to draw attention to the wide range of meaning covered by such expressions as "the light within," and "the inner or inward light."

Both by our Master Himself, and by the Friends who originally preached Him as the Light, the figure of light was used in a broad and popular sense. Light is the most obvious and the most eternally satisfying figure for Divine truth. It is, however, hardly more obvious or more satisfying than the other figure so commonly, and almost interchangeably, used by the same teachers, of breath—inspiration. I scarcely know whether it would convey most truth to say that the corner stone of our Society was a belief in "the light within," or in "immediate inspiration." I doubt whether the two ideas are in all respects altogether distinguishable. Belief in the fact to which they both refer, of an actual Divine influence communicated to every human spirit, is our real corner-stone.*

° I may, perhaps, here be allowed to point out the ambiguity of the expression "immediate inspiration." The word "immediate" may be understood to mean direct, and in this sense it is, I think, superfluous; for it is surely impossible to conceive of inspiration as indirect, although revelation may easily

The fact of inspiration is denied by no Christian—
the full recognition of its present and constant operation
is in some degree a peculiarity of Friends. It is not
uncommon outside the Society to hear expressions
implying that Divine inspiration is a thing of the past:
a quite exceptional gift, familiar only in apostolic
times. It seems to me that this limitation of its range
amounts almost to a denial of its reality. I can hardly
understand the idea that God did occasionally long ago
speak to human beings, but that He never does so now.
It seems, at any rate, inconsistent with any worthy
sense of His unchangeableness.

Many of us have come to believe that one of the
greatest hindrances to a real belief in or recognition of
inspiration has been the exceedingly crude and
mechanical conception of it as attributed to the letter
of scripture. From this hard and shallow way of
thinking about inspiration, Friends have generally been
preserved in proportion as they have held firmly the

---

be so. But it may also, in reference to any particular thought
communicated, be understood as meaning " instantaneous "; and
in this sense a special importance has been attached to it by some
Friends, which is, I believe, deprecated by others, as restricting
" ministry " to the utterance of words believed to be at the
moment given for utterance, under what is called a " fresh
annointing " from above. I would, therefore, rather avoid at
present the use of the expression " immediate inspiration," when
speaking of our belief that there is in every heart a witness for
the truth, which is, so to speak radiated from the central truth.
The " light " seems, on the whole, to be the figure least open to any
possible misinterpretation.

old Quaker doctrine of the light within. Some, no
doubt, have gone too far in the direction of transferring
the idea of infallibility from the Bible to themselves.
But, on the whole, I believe the doctrine of Fox and
Barclay (*i.e.*, briefly, that the " Word of God " is Christ,
not the Bible, and that the Scriptures are profitable in
proportion as they are read in the same spirit which
gave them forth) to have been a most valuable equipoise
to the tendency of other Protestant sects to transfer the
idea of infallibility from the Church to the Bible.
Nothing, I believe, can really teach us the nature and
meaning of inspiration but personal experience of it.
That we may all have such experience if we will but
attend to the Divine influences in our own hearts, is
the cardinal doctrine of Quakerism. Whether this
belief, honestly acted on, will manifest itself in the
homespun and solid, but only too sober morality of
the typical everyday Quaker, or whether it will land
us in the mystical fervours of an Isaac Penington, or
the apostolic labours of a John Woolman or a Stephen
Grellet, must depend chiefly upon our natural temperament and special gifts. The range of the different
forms taken by the doctrine is as wide as the range of
human endowment and experience. A belief which is
the common property of the prophet and the babe will,
of course, yield every variety of practical result.

It is a belief which it is hardly possible to inculcate
by anything more or less than a direct appeal to
experience, to the witness within ; and there is the
further difficulty, that the experience to which we can
appeal only as sharers in it, must be expressed in

language very often and very naturally misunderstood. The assertion, however guarded, that one has actual experience of Divine inspiration in one's own person, is very apt to sound like a claim to personal infallibility. Yet in reality nothing can be further from the mark. The first effect of the shining of light within is to show what is amiss—to "convince of sin." It is not claiming any superiority to ordinary human conditions to say, in response to such an appeal as that of the Friends just referred to, "Yes, I have indeed been conscious of a power within making manifest to me my sins and errors, and I have indeed experienced its healing and emancipating power as well as its fiery purgings and bitter condemnations. That which has shown me my fault has healed me; the light has led and is leading me onwards and upwards out of the abyss, nearer and nearer to its own eternal Source; and I know that, in so far as I am obedient to it, I am safe." What is such a reply but an acknowledgment that "the light, the Spirit, and grace of Christ" have indeed been an indwelling, in-breathing power in one's own heart? If it be a claim to inspiration, it is a claim which implies no merit and no eminence in him who makes it; it is made on ground common to the publican, the prodigal, and the sinner, to Magdalen and to Paul. It is the history of every child returning to the Father's house.

But it is not every one to whom it would be natural to describe this experience in language so mystical as this, nor would the mystic's experience be likely to stop short at anything so simple and elementary as the process just described. And here we are confronted

with the real " peculiarity" of Quakerism—its relation
to mysticism. There is no doubt that George Fox
himself and the other fathers of the Society were of a
strongly mystical turn of mind, though not in the sense
in which the word is often used by the worshippers
of "common sense," as a mild term of reproach, to
convey a general vague dreaminess. Nothing, certainly,
could be less applicable to the early Friends than any
such reproach as this. They were fiery, dogmatic,
pugnacious, and intensely practical and sober-minded·
But they were assuredly mystics in what I take to be
the more accurate sense of that word—people, that is,
with a vivid consciousness of the inwardness of the
light of truth.

Mysticism in this sense is a well-known phenomenon,
of which a multitude of examples may be found in all
religions. It is, indeed, rather a personal peculiarity
than a form of belief; and therefore, although from
time to time associations (our own, for one) have been
based upon what are called mystical tenets, there can
scarcely be anything like a real school of mysticism—
at any rate in Europe. Mysticism, as we know it, is
essentially individual. It refuses to be formulated or
summed up. In one sense it is common to all religious
persuasions; in another, it equally eludes them all.
We can easily understand what constitutes a mystic,
but the peculiarity itself is incommunicable. Their
belief is an open secret. They themselves have ever
desired to communicate it, though continually feeling
the impossibility of doing so by words alone. It is the
secret of light—an inward light clothing itself in life,

and living to bring all things to the light.   Mystics, as
I understand the matter, are those whose minds, to
their own consciousness, are lighted from within : who
feel themselves, that is, to be in immediate inward
communication with the central Fountain of light and
life.   They have naturally a vivid sense both of the
distinction and of the harmony between the inward
and the outward—a sense so vivid that it is impossible
for them to believe it to be unshared by others.   A true
mystic believes that all men have, as he himself is conscious of having, an inward life, into which, as into a
secret chamber, he can retreat at will.°   In this inner
chamber he finds a refuge from the ever-changing
aspects of outward existence ; from the multitude of
cares and pleasures and agitations which belong to the
life of the senses and the affections ; from human
judgments ; from all change, and chance, and turmoil,
and distraction.   He finds there, first repose, then an
awful guidance ; a light which burns and purifies ; a
voice which subdues ; he finds himself in the presence
of his God.   It is here, in this holy of holies, that
"deep calleth unto deep:" here that the imperishable,
unfathomable, unchanging elements of humanity meet

° Let me not be understood to mean that the process of "keeping the mind" (in Quaker phrase) "retired to the Lord" is an
easy one. On the contrary it may need strenuous effort. But
the *effort* can be made at will, and even the mere effort thus to
retire from the surface to the depths of life is sure to bring help
and strengthening—is in itself a strengthening, steadying
process.

and are one with the Divine Fountain of life from whence they flow : here that the well of living waters springeth up unto eternal life.

" The kingdom of heaven is within you." Personal religion is a real and a living thing only in proportion as it springs from this deep inward root. The root itself is common to all true believers. The consciousness of its "inwardness" is that which distinguishes the mystic. How it should be that to some minds the words " inward and outward " express the most vivid and continuous fact of consciousness, while to others they appear to have no meaning at all ; how it comes that some are born mystics, while to others the report of the mystic concerning the inner life is a thing impossible to be believed and hardly to be understood :— these are psychological problems I cannot attempt to unravel. If, however, a certain correspondence between the inward and outward do really exist (and this I suppose will hardly be denied, whatever may be the most philosophically accurate way of expressing it), the faculty of discerning it must needs be a gift. I believe, indeed, that the power in this direction which distinguishes such mystics as, *e.g.*, Thomas à Kempis, Jacob Boehme, Tauler, Fénélon, Madame Guyon, George Fox, William Law, St. Theresa, Molinos, and others is essentially the same gift which in a different form, or in combination with a different temperament and gifts of another order, makes poets. It is the gift of seeing truth at first-hand, the faculty of receiving a direct revelation. Yet to have an eye to see " the light which lighteth every man that cometh into the world " is to be assured that it is the common inheritance. Preachers like those I have just mentioned always appeal to it with confidence as to a witness to be found in every heart. And surely experience confirms this conviction of theirs. It is in degree only that their gift is exceptional. They may have the sight of an eagle, but they see by the same light as the bat.

Now the obvious tendency of a vivid first-hand perception of truth, or light, is to render the possessor of it so far independent of external teachers. And we all know that in point of fact such *illuminati* always have shown a disposition to go their own way, and to disregard, if not to denounce, traditional teaching, which has brought them into frequent collisions with ecclesiastical and other authorities. Those of the Church of Rome, have, with their wonted sagacity, as much as possible sought to turn this strange power to account, while providing safety-valves for the unmanageable residue.

It is the easier to do this because of the two marked characteristics of mystics—quietness and independence. Mystics are naturally independent, not only of ecclesiastical authority, but of each other. This is necessarily implied in the very idea of first-hand reception of light. While it must always constitute a strong bond of sympathy between those who recognize it in themselves and in each other, it naturally indisposes them to discipleship. They sit habitually at no man's feet, and do not as a rule greatly care to have anyone sit at theirs. Mysticism in this sense seems naturally opposed to tradition. No true mystic would hold himself bound by the thoughts of others. He does not feel the need of them, being assured of the sufficiency and conscious of the possession of that inward guidance, whether called light, or voice, or inspiration, which must be seen, heard, felt, by each one in his own heart, or not at all. But the duty of looking for and of obeying this guidance is a principle which may be inculcated and transmitted from generation to generation like any other principle. Its hereditary influence is very perceptible in old Quaker families, where a unique type of Christian character resulting from it is still to be met with.

Quietness naturally accompanies the belief in this inward guidance, not only because in the Divine presence all that is merely human necessarily sinks into silent insignificance, but also because it is instinctively felt that it is only in stillness that any perfect reflection from above can be formed in the mirror of the human spirit. The natural fruit of mysticism is quietism.

I have no means of estimating the actual prevalence of mystical and quietist principles in the Society of Friends at the present time. But I am sure that our Society is the natural home for the spirits of all those who hold them, for it is the one successful embodiment of these principles in a system of " Church government." Every arrangement is made to favour and to maintain the practice of looking for individual inward guidance, and to give the freest scope to its results. Everything which tends to hinder obedience to it is abandoned and discouraged. I shall endeavour to trace the working of this aim in various special directions hereafter. I must now endeavour to explain as well as I can what it is precisely that I understand by that inward light, voice, or Divine guidance which we Friends believe it our duty and our highest privilege in all things to watch for.

I do not, indeed, claim that my own share in this deepest region of human experience amounts to more than a faint and intermittent glimmering of what I know to be possible. I earnestly desire to explain to others what to myself has been especially blessed and helpful in the deepest unfoldings, whether by word or in life, of Quaker principles ; but I feel that the task would demand for its full accomplishment not only greater powers than mine, but also the assistance which can be given only by something more than candour in the reader—by a real desire to help out the stammering utterance, and to supply the gaps left by individual shortcomings. To such a helpful auditor, therefore, I will in imagination address myself.

Faithfulness to the light is the watchword of all who hunger and thirst after righteousness—of all seekers after the kingdom of heaven. Is this merely an equivalent for the more commonplace expression, " obedience to conscience " ? Surely not. Conscience, as we all know, is liable to perversion, to morbid exaggerations, to partial insensibility, to twists and crotchets of all sorts, and itself needs correction by various external standards. Conscience, therefore, can never be our supreme and absolute guide. Whether it can ever be right to disobey it, must depend on the precise meaning we attach to the words "conscience" and "right," and into this puzzle I have no intention of entering. In a broad and practical sense, we all know that if there were nothing above conscience, conscience would assuredly lead many of us into the ditch : nay, that, for want of enlightenment from above, it actually has led many there. The light by which our consciences must be enlightened, the light in obedience to which is our supreme good, must be something purer than this fallible faculty itself. It must be that power within us, if any such power there be, which is one with all the wisdom, all the goodness, all the order and harmony, without us ; one with "the power, not ourselves, which makes for righteousness"; one with "the eternal will towards all goodness." It must be a power as all-pervading and immanent in the spirit of man as is the power of gravity (or whatever yet more elementary force gravity may be resolved into) in the outer world he inhabits. It must be the power in which we live and move and have our being —the power and the presence of God.

I do not attempt—idle indeed would be the attempt in such hands as mine—to contribute anything towards the arguments in favour of Theism. To those who do not believe in the existence of the living God, the whole subject upon which I am engaged must be without interest or significance. And I leave it to others to reconcile, or to show that we need not attempt to reconcile, the existence of evil with the omnipotence of God. The mystery in which all our searchings after a complete theory concerning the Author of our being must needs lose themselves need not perplex, though it may overshadow, those practical questions as to our own right attitude towards Him with which alone I am concerned. I assume faith in Him and allegiance to Him as the very ground under our feet ; if this be not granted, it is idle to go further. My reason for going so far even as I have done in this direction (the direction, I mean, of inquiring into our fundamental assumptions) is that I cannot help thinking that our Quaker faith respecting immediate Divine guidance rests upon a wider basis of common conviction than is usually supposed. I believe it to be the legitimate, though by no means the frequent, result of any sincere belief in God, however attained — not merely an outgrowth from one peculiar form of Christianity. The coldest and most cautious Theist can say no less than that God does in some sense direct the course of this world and of all that is in it. The most ecstatic mystic can bear witness to nothing beyond the fact that God does in deed and in truth pervade and sway the inmost recesses of his own being. Is not this the very same truth, seen under the magnifying and amplifying power of first-hand experience ?

To me it seems idle to attempt to find any resting-place between convinced atheism on the one hand, and absolute self-surrender to the indwelling influence of the Divine Spirit on the other ; the barrier, if there be any barrier, is surely not so much a logical as a moral hindrance. Believing in God, and worshipping Him with one's whole heart, trusting Him absolutely and loving Him supremely, seem to me to be but various stages in the growth of one seed. I know, alas! but too well, that this growth is slow, and that it meets with obstacles and checks at every moment. I know that our faith has not only to struggle, but to struggle through the darkness, and that it may be challenged at every step by difficulties which it cannot solve. But I cannot admit that there is any consistency or reason in treading the path of faith half-way. I cannot admit that it is reasonable to believe in God as the Supreme Being, and unreasonable to seek His living presence and direction in the minutest details of our everyday life. With Him, surely, our distinctions of great and small disappear, and "the darkness is no darkness at all." "Whither shall I go then from Thy presence? If I go down into hell, and remain in the uttermost parts of the earth, even there shall Thy hand lead me, and Thy right hand shall hold me."

But many will say, This may all be quite true, but how are we to distinguish between the voice of God and the many other voices which distract our attention from it? How, if God is everywhere, does the practical result differ from His being nowhere? To the full extent of my ability I recognize this great difficulty. It seems to throw us back for guidance upon those very powers whose insufficiency we have just recognized. If I reply, God is to be recognized in "whatsoever things are true, whatsoever things are pure, and lovely, and of good report," you may well retort, And how, except through our fallible consciences, shall we discern truth, purity, loveliness?

I believe that the difficulty of distinguishing between

the will, or the voice, or the light of God, and the wills
and voices and lights of a lower kind from which it is
to be distinguished, is not only not to be ignored, but
that the very first step towards learning the lesson is to
recognize that it is a lesson, and a hard one—nay, a
lifelong discipline. But just as the child trusts instinctively, absolutely, helplessly, before it has even
begun to attempt to understand its parents, so, surely,
we may and must trust God first and unreservedly,
before we begin slowly and feebly, yet perseveringly,
to acquaint ourselves with Him. And as the trust of
the full-grown son or daughter is a nobler thing than
the trust of the infant, so the experience of wisdom and
prudence has doubtless a revelation of its own—a
precious addition to that essential revelation which is
made in the first place to babes, and to the wise only
in so far as they too have childlike hearts. To have
our senses exercised to discern between truth and false-
hood, light and darkness, order and disorder, the will
of God and the will of the flesh, is, I believe, the end
and object of our training in this world. There is no
royal road to it. Yet can we honestly say that it is
impossible?

If, then, it is only by a slow and gradual process that
we can rise to anything like a true knowledge (even
according to our human measure) of God, must it not
be by a slow and gradual process alone that He can
make His voice and His guiding touch distinguishable
by us and intelligible to us? Is it any wonder if those
who do not attribute to Him so much as the broad
obvious laws by which we are all hedged in from gross

wrong-doing and error, should fail to recognize the reality or the significance of those delicate restraining touches by which the spirits which yield themselves to His care are moulded into some faint likeness to the Son of His love ? Must not the first step towards entering into the meaning of that which is personal and individual be the acceptance of what is equally applicable to all ?*

That individual and immediate guidance, in which we recognise that "the finger of God is come unto us," seems to come in, as it were, to complete and perfect the work rough-hewn by morality and conscience. We may liken the laws of our country to the cliffs of our island, over which we rarely feel ourselves in any danger of falling : the moral standard of our social circle to the beaten highway road which we can hardly miss. Our own conscience would then be represented by a fence, by which some parts of the country are enclosed for each one, the road itself at times barred or narrowed. And that Divine guidance of which I am speaking could be typified only by the pressure of a hand upon ours, leading us gently to step to the right or the left, to pause or to go forward, in a manner intended for and understood by ourselves alone.†

---

* ": If ye have not been faithful in that which is another man's who shall give you that which is your own ?" (Luke xvi. 12).

† I do not, of course, forget that, owing to the imperfection of human laws, and human faculties, cases may and do occur in which Divine guidance may lead us in ways which run counter to them. The figure used above is intended only to illustrate the general

When I say I have been "rightly guided" to this or that step, I mean that being well within the limits prescribed by morality, by personal claims, by the closest attention to the voice of conscience, I have yet felt that there was still a choice to be made as between things equally innocent but probably not equally excellent—a choice, perhaps, between different levels almost infinitely remote from each other—and that in making that choice I have acted under an impelling or restraining power not of my own exerting. I generally mean, further, that in making the choice I have looked, and probably asked, for light from above, and that the results of such choice have tended to confirm the belief that my action has been prompted by One who could see the end from the beginning, who knew things hidden from myself, and "understood my path long before" : in short, that I have been led as the blind by a way I knew not. Is not such experience as this witnessed to by multitudes of Christians, especially as

correspondence between the map, as it were, which can be laid down by the reason of man, and that individual and immediate guidance which alone can show us a higher and a narrower, but yet freer, pathway—the pathway of that highest service which is perfect freedom. When in exceptional cases, any contrariety really emerges between the human and the Divine guiding lines, we may surely still, without too much straining of our figure, say that it is a living power only which can free any human spirit from the too narrow fencing in of a morbid and unenlightened conscience, and guide it by paths running counter to the beaten track of conventional morality, or even in some rare instances authorize and enable and require it to overleap even the cliffs of actual law, trusting that in such cases, as experience has already taught us, the blood of the martyrs will still be the seed of the Church.

they advance in life? For it may take long years of patience before the last pieces are fitted into the puzzle, so as to enable us to judge of the intention of the whole.

I am well aware that I am speaking of a region of experience in which there is abundant room for self-deception. I know that those who, out of the abundance of the heart, speak very freely of these things with their lips are apt not only to shock one's sense of reverence, but to betray a deplorable want of logic in the inferences they draw from trifling facts—facts whose significance to themselves cannot possibly be conveyed to others, and may indeed very likely be in large measure fanciful or even distorted. I think that we are wrong when we attempt to found any sort of proof or argument in favour of what is called "a particular providence" exclusively upon the occurrences of our own lives. People forget that what is most convincing to themselves, because it was within the four walls of their own experience that it happened, is for that very reason least convincing to others—that is, in the way of argument, though the *impression* may, of course, be sympathetically shared, and may rightly have special weight with those who have reason to trust the speaker. But, as a general rule, I believe that reverence and reason combine to demand that the personal and intimate dealings of Divine Providence with each one should be mainly reserved for personal and intimate use and edification. Proof or argument as to the general truth that God does guide His people individually must be founded upon a wider basis than

is afforded by any one person's experience. I believe
that there are abundant reasons, of a far-reaching and
deep kind, to justify each one in looking for the
minutest individual guidance. I cannot, indeed, as I
have already said, understand how those who believe
in a providential order at all can limit it to the
larger outlines, or, as is so often done in practice, to the
pleasing results of the Divine government. If we
believe, in any real and honest sense, that the ordering
of all human affairs is in the hands of one supreme
Ruler, how can we stop short of believing that the
minuest trifle affecting any one of us is under the
same all-pervading care? It would, I think, be as
reasonable to say that God created animals, but left it
to each one to develop its own fur or feathers. And,
again, if we attribute our preservation from danger to
Him, how can we flinch from the parallel belief that
by His ordinance also we were exposed to it; yes, and
in some cases doomed to suffer the worst it can wreak
upon us, "without reprieve"?

Therefore I believe that, before we can hope to enter
into that intimate and blessed communion with God
which transfigures all life, two great conditions must
be fulfilled. We must have settled it in our hearts
that everything, from the least to the greatest, is to be
taken as His language—language which it is our main
business here to learn to interpret—and we must be
willing to face all pain as His discipline.

I know, of course, that these two conditions can be
perfectly fulfilled only as the result of much dicipline
and much experience of the very guidance in question.

But their roots—docility and courage—are in some measure implanted in us long before we begin to think about such questions as the government of the world or the ordering of our lives.

It is, I believe, in the last of these two demands of logic, the demand upon our courage, that the moral hindrance to a full belief in Divine guidance mainly lies. People cannot bring themselves to *feel* that the infliction of pain can be the act of One whom they desire to know as Love. Yet this is the very central demand of Christianity. What is courage but the willingness to encounter suffering, the readiness to take up the cross?

In the strength of the Spirit of Christ, the everlasting Son of the Father, we *can* rise to this victory of trust; we can meet life without flinching, and read its darkest riddles in the light of the revelation of Divine love which he has won for us by His own suffering and death. Seen in that light, it is, according to the universal testimony of the saints, a gentle though often most severe, unfolding of depth within depth of heavenly wisdom—gentle beyond words in its methods, yet inexorable in its conditions. At every step the fiery baptism must be encountered. The deep things of God cannot be reached except through the very destruction of the perishing flesh. It is through death that we enter into life. But as we do enter into it, we can truly look back and say that His ordering has been better than our planning—that His thoughts are high above our thoughts, as the heaven is above the earth.

Our goal must be a heavenly one if we are to judge

truly of His guidance. The home to which, if we trust Him, He will assuredly lead us, is no earthly home: but Zion—the heavenly Jerusalem: the beautiful city of peace, which can be entered only through much tribulation. Those who are looking for smooth roads and luxurious resting-places may well say they perceive no sign of guidance at all. The Divine guidance is away from self-indulgence, often away from outward success: through humiliation and failure, and many snares and temptations: over rough roads and against opposing forces—always uphill. Its evidence of success is in the inmost, deepest, most spiritual part of our experience. It is idle indeed to talk of it to those whose faces are not set Zionwards. It will bring them none of the results in which they have their reward. Those who know the voice of the Divine Guide, and those who deny that it can be heard, are not so much contradicting each other as speaking different languages —or rather speaking in reference to different states of existence.

I have been speaking of "light," "voice," "guidance," as almost equivalent and interchangeable expressions for our consciousness of the presence of God with us and in us. In the expression "inspiration" we have further the symbol of His power—of the upbearing, purifying, energizing gift of His own Spirit. Here words almost fail: and fresh care is needed, whether in speaking or in hearing, as we draw near to those depths which "cannot be uttered." I pause on the threshold of the inner chamber of the heart, the holy place of true worship.

CHAPTER III.

WORSHIP.

OUR manner of worship is the natural (as it seems to me even the inevitable) result of the full recognition of the reality of Divine inspiration—of the actual living present sufficient fulness of intercourse between the human spirit and Him who is the Father of spirits. Who that truly expects to hear the voice of God can do otherwise than bow in silence before Him ?

" Devotion," says Bishop Butler in one of his sermons,* " is retirement from the world He has made, to Him alone : it is to withdraw from the avocations of sense, *to yield ourselves up to the influences of the Divine presence*, and to give full scope to the affections of gratitude, love, reverence, trust, and dependence : of which infinite Power, Wisdom, and Goodness is the natural and only Object." No words could more fully

---

* Sermon XIV., " On the Love of God," Butler's " Sermons," p. 278 (London, 1726). And in his charge to the clergy of Durham, published with the " Analogy " (London, 1802), he repeats the words which I have printed above in italics, and speaks of public worship as " a time of devotion, when we are assembled to yield ourselves up to the full influence of the Divine presence."

or worthily express the intention of a Friends' meeting—of one of those " meetings for worship " which are, as is well known, "held on a basis of silence," but in which free course is allowed to whatever Divine influence may prompt of vocal prayer, preaching, testimony, or prophecy ; those meetings in which each one, it is felt, should in the first place enter into the inmost sanctuary of his own heart, and be alone with God ; being still, that His voice may be clearly heard within, before the lips can rightly be opened to show forth His praise or His counsels to others. From the depths of that stillness words do from time to time arise—words uttered in simple obedience to the upspringing of the fountain from within. This is what we mean by being " moved by the Spirit," and I do not see how a worthier or a truer expression could be found for the perfect ideal of spiritual worship.

That mysterious diversity which is interwoven with all our likeness, and belongs to the very nature common to us all makes it impossible for one to judge for another as to the manner of worship most likely to be vitally helpful to him. I cannot tell how far my own feeling about Friends' meetings may arise from an idiosyncrasy. I do not pretend to feel, as did some of the early Friends, that all pre-arrangement is in itself unlawful or sinful. I can well understand the point of view of those who believe that the majestic and time-hallowed words of such a Liturgy as the Anglican afford the nearest approach to a worthy manner of public worship. I can even understand, though with less of sympathy, the feelings of those who dread lest the utterances of their untutored fellow-worshippers should disturb their own endeavours to attain to a devotional frame of mind. But though for these and other reasons, I am prepared to admit that the extreme of simplicity and freedom maintained in our own meetings might not prove helpful to everyone, and though I have no desire to conceal the too obvious fact that we continually fall very far short of our ideal, I yet must avow my own conviction that that ideal of public worship is the purest which has ever been recognised, and also that it is practically identical with that which seems to have been recognized in the days of the apostles. I further believe that there are many, in these days especially, to whom it is the one manner of worship which is still practically possible, as being absolutely free from anything entangling to the conscience, or open to controversy. I have already* spoken of the indescribable relief which it afforded to my own mind, at a time when I was sorely harassed by difficulties—common to how many in these days !—as to the sincerity of appropriating for my own use forms which, however beautiful, are open to so much and such serious question. What I felt I wanted in a place of worship was a refuge, or at least the opening of a door-way towards the refuge, from doubts and controversies ; not a fresh encounter with them. Yet it seems to me impossible that any one harassed by the conflicting views of truth with which just now the air is thick, should be able to forget controversy while listening to

---

° See Introduction.

such language as that of the Book of Common Prayer. It seems to me that nothing but silence can heal the wounds made by disputations in the region of the unseen. No external help, at any rate, has ever in my own experience proved so penetratingly efficacious as the habit of joining in a public worship based upon silence. Its primary attraction for me was in the fact that it pledged me to nothing, and left me altogether undisturbed to seek for help in my own way. But before long I began to be aware that the united and prolonged silences had a far more direct and powerful effect than this. They soon began to exercise a strangely subduing and softening effect upon my mind. There used, after a while, to come upon me a deep sense of awe, as we sat together and waited—for what? In my heart of hearts I knew in whose Name we were met together, and who was truly in the midst of us. Never before had His influence revealed itself to me with so much power as in those quiet assemblies.

And another result of the practice of silent waiting for the unseen Presence proved to be a singularly effectual preparation of mind for the willing reception of any words which might be offered "in the name of a disciple." The words spoken were indeed often feeble, and always inadequate (as all words must be in relation to Divine things), sometimes even entirely irrelevant to my own individual needs, though at other times profoundly impressive and helpful; but, coming as they did after the long silences which had fallen like dew upon the thirsty soil, they went far deeper, and were received into a much less thorny region than had

ever been the case with the words I had listened to
from the pulpit.

In Friends' meetings also, from the fact that every
one is free to speak, one hears harmonies and correspondences between very various utterances such as are
scarcely to be met with elsewhere. It is sometimes as
part-singing compared with unison. The free admission
of the ministry of women, of course, greatly enriches
this harmony. I have often wondered whether some
of the motherly counsels I have listened to in our
meeting would not reach some hearts that might be
closed to the masculine preacher.

But it is not only the momentary effect of silence as
a help in public worship that constitutes its importance
in Quaker estimation. The silence we value is not the
mere outward silence of the lips. It is a deep quietness of heart and mind, a laying aside of all preoccupation with passing things—yes, even with the
workings of our own minds; a resolute fixing of the
heart upon that which is unchangeable and eternal.
This " silence of all flesh " appears to us to be the
essential preparation for any act of true worship. It is
also, we believe, the essential condition at all times of
inward illumination. " Stand still in the light," says
George Fox again and again, and then strength comes
—and peace and victory and deliverance, and all other
good things. " Be still, and know that I am God." It
is the experience, I believe, of all those who have been
most deeply conscious of His revelations of Himself,
that they are made emphatically to the " waiting " soul
—to the spirit which is most fully conscious of its own

inability to do more than wait in silence before Him. The possibilities of inward silence can be but distantly referred to in words. The clearness of inward vision which sometimes results from it must be experienced to be fully understood ; the things revealed to that vision are rather to be lived in than uttered. But the fact that a strenuous endeavour to lay aside all disturbing influences, and to allow all external vibrations to subside, is an important, if not an essential, preparation for the reception of eternal truth, seems to be indisputable. To be quiet must surely always be a gain. To rule one's own spirit, and to acquire the power of proclaiming at least a truce within, must surely be recognized by the least " mystical " as a rational and wholesome exercise of self-control.

It is, to my own mind, a singular confirmation of the depth of truth in the Quaker ideal, that it embraces in its application such widely varying degrees of spirituality. The " inward silence " which to the mystic means the gateway of the unspeakable, the limpid calmness of the mirror in which heaven's glory is to be reflected, commends itself also to the sternest rationalist as the beginning of fortitude. And the experience of some of us (whom I may, perhaps, venture to describe as rational mystics) proves the exceeding value of the habit of seeking after inward silence as a real life-discipline. Not only at the times set apart for definite acts of worship—though, whether in public or in private, it is from the heart of this stillness that the voice of deepest prayer and praise springs up—but also in all the daily warfare of the Christian life, in en-

countering joy or sorrow, temptation or perplexity, the
first condition and the highest reward of victory is
equanimity. " Be not thou greatly moved " ; " Fret
not thyself, else shalt thou be moved to do evil." There
is no need to multiply the words of the wise on this
head. We all surely have gone through times when
" he opened not his lips " expresses the only possible
attitude in which we can hope to win through. Silence
and resolution, indeed, seem almost like different
aspects of the same thing. And silence is assuredly an
art to be acquired, a discipline to be steadily practised,
before it can become the instinctive habit and unfailing
resource of the soul. The wise Roman Catholic teachers
all enjoin this discipline upon those who desire to learn
" perfection." Friends inculcate it rather by example
than by precept, though abundant recognition of its
importance is to be found in Quaker writings. But I
am specially concerned with the practical results of our
manner of worship ; and I am bound to say that, to
myself, the practice of quietness in life is markedly
facilitated by the habit of joining in a worship " based
on silence."

The connection between our practice of silence and
our belief in inspiration is, I think, obvious. , How can
we listen if we do not cease to speak ? How can we
receive while we maintain an incessant activity ? It is
obvious that " a wise passiveness " is essential to the
possibility of serving as channels for any Divinely
given utterance. On this subject of being " moved by
the Spirit," there seems often to be the strangest difficulty in people's minds. They imagine that Friends

claim the possession of something like a miraculous gift
—something as baffling to ordinary reason as the speaking in unknown tongues of the Irvingites. Speaking
under correction, and with a sense that the matter
reaches to unknown depths, I should say that this was
quite a mistake. What Friends undoubtedly believe
and maintain is that to the listening heart God does
speak intelligibly ; and further, that some amongst
His worshippers are gifted with a special openness to
receive and power to transmit in words, actual messages
from Himself. Is this more than is necessarily implied
in the belief that real communion with Him is not
only possible, but is freely open to all ?

We do not regard those who have the gift of
" ministry " as infallible, or even as necessarily closer
to God than many of the silent worshippers who form
the great majority in every congregation. We feel
that the gift is from above, and that on all of us lies
the responsibility of being open to it, willing to receive
it, should it be bestowed, and to use it faithfully while
entrusted with it. But we fully recognize that to do
this perfectly requires a continual submission of the
will, and an unceasing watchfulness. We know that
to " keep close to the gift " is not an easy thing. We
know that the singleness of eye which alone can enable
any one always to discern between the immediate
guidance of the Divine Spirit and the mere promptings
of our own hearts, is not attained without much
patience, and a diligent and persevering use of all the
means of instruction provided for us. We recognize
the value of such corrections even as may come

through the minds of others ; for, although the servant is responsible only to his own Master, and we desire earnestly to beware of any dependence on each other in such matters, yet it has (as I have already mentioned) been thought right that some Friends should be specially appointed to watch over the ministers in the exercise of their gift. The "elders," to whom this task is entrusted, do in fact often offer not only encouragement or counsel, but at times admonition and even rebuke, when they believe it to be needed. It is thus clear that the Society has always held with the Apostle Paul that "the spirits of the prophets are subject to the prophets." The great care and caution shown in all the arrangements of the Society with respect to ministry bear witness to its recognition of the deep truth, that the more precious the treasure, the more serious the risks to which the earthen vessels enclosing it are exposed.

The question is often asked, How can you distinguish between a message from above and the suggestions of your own imagination ? * The only answer which

---

* It is I think, in this connection important to distinguish between the question, How do you in practice distinguish between a true and a false message ? and the quite separate inquiry, How do you in theory distinguish between the human faculty of imagination and the Divine action signified by the word "inspiration"? It is with the first question only that I have been concerned in the text, as it is, I believe, the only question with which honesty requires us to grapple. Any attempt to give a full answer to the second question would require a degree of

can be given to this question is, that to do so for practical purposes does indeed require all the heavenly wisdom and all the humble sincerity of heart of which we are capable. Worship, to those who believe that God is, and is indeed to be worshipped in spirit and in truth, is surely the highest function of the human spirit. To attain to such a transparency of heart and mind as shall admit of our serving as channels for the worship of others, and for the Divine response to such worship—ladders, as it were, on which the angels of God may ascend and descend in the place of worship—is, indeed, an aim which must transcend all merely human power. We need for it the continual renovation of Him who is Light—"the Way, the Truth, and the Life." But dare any, who call themselves believers on Him, doubt that such renovation is open to us?

I can understand those who think all worship idle, or worse than idle! I cannot understand those who think it can be acceptably performed without the help of the Spirit Himself making intercession for us, and

---

pyschological skill to which I have no claim ; and I doubt whether the very terms of the question do not lead us beyond the province even of psychology. But, speaking in a popular and trustful way, I should reply that we are not concerned to discern the precise limits of the Divine and the human ; only to throw open the deepest human powers to the purest Divine influences ; that the result we look for is the fruit of a devout intelligence, first purified, and then swayed, by the immediate action of Divine power. It surely involves something like a contradiction in terms to inquire at what precise line a distinction is obliterated ?

with us and in us, or that this help will fail any true worshipper. Yet, if we do believe this help is given, are we not looking to be "moved by the Spirit"? Is the expectation peculiar to any one body of Christians? Surely not. What *is* peculiar to us Friends is the dread of limiting or interfering with the immediate influences of the Divine Spirit by the use of fixed forms of words or by outward observances or pressure of any kind.

As I have already said, I do not feel that ours is the only lawful manner of worship ; I do not even think it at all clear that it would be for all people and at all times the most helpful. But I do believe it to be the purest conceivable. I am jealous for its preservation from any admixture of adventitious "aids to devotion." I believe that its absolute freedom and flexibility, its unrivalled simplicity and gravity, make it a vessel of honour prepared in an especial manner for the conveyance of the pure water of life to many in these days who are hindered from satisfying their souls' thirst by questionable additions to the essence of Divine worship.

I know that, in Friends' meetings as elsewhere, one must be prepared to meet with much human weakness and imperfection ; many things may be heard in them which are trying to the flesh—yes, and perhaps to the spirit also. Certainly many things may be heard which are open to criticism from an intellectual and literary point of view. Let no one go to Friends' meetings with the expectation of finding everything to his taste. Yet even mere taste, if duly cultivated, must recognize the value of a certain weight and simplicity, arising no doubt, from the habitual practice of inward silence, by which they are often distinguished. This is, however, a point upon which no one who is alive to the real significance of such meetings as ours would care to dwell. Criticism fades away abashed in the presence of what is felt to be a real, however faltering, endeavour to open actual communication with the Father of spirits, and with each other as in His presence and in His name. To my own mind, any living utterance to a human voice pleading for itself and for the objects of its love in words fresh from the heart, has a power and a pathos infinitely beyond that of the most perfect expression of devotion read or recited according to an appointed order.*

It is an important peculiarity of our meetings that the responsibility for their character is felt to be shared by all. I do not mean that all our members are in fact alive to their own share of this responsibility. The service is, no doubt, often far too much left to one or more willing speakers. But I do not believe that it

---

* People have said to me again and again, if you want to be silent, why cannot you be silent at home? Such an objection seems hardly intended to be seriously answered, yet I have heard it so often that I cannot but notice it. Surely it need hardly be pointed out that it applies at least equally strongly to the practice of meeting together to join in prayers, which, being already in print and chosen according to the calendar, each of us might read at home. But the worthier answer is that, whether our utterance be prearranged or spontaneous, we meet in order to kindle in each other the flame of true worship, and also to show forth our allegiance to the Master, in whom we are so united as to feel our need of each other's sympathy in drawing near to Him.

would be possible amongst Friends for anything like the sense of dependence on one individual to arise which seems naturally to result from the idea of a priestly order. And, at any rate, the ideal is kept continually before us of a company coming together on one level, each of whom is free and encouraged to bring his individual offering of praise and prayer, whether silent or vocal. It is a familiar thought amongst Friends that no one should expect in a meeting for worship "to eat the bread of idleness." And the practice which is so frequent amongst us of ministering Friends travelling from meeting to meeting in the exercise of their gift, causes a stirring of the waters and keeps up the sense of the freedom of all to take their part whenever and wherever a word may be given them.

There is one other result of the absence of pre-arrangement in our meetings which I cannot altogether pass over. It is that no shelter is provided under cover of which one can remain in doubt whether one is or is not actually engaged in worship on one's own account. A liturgy or a hymn may bear along in its current many a vague half-formed tendency towards worship: and I dare not say that it may not thus sometimes fan the spark into a flame, or save the smoking flax from being altogether quenched. But it does seem to me that it also often prevents our recognizing our own poverty, and stifles many an individual cry for help which the sense of that poverty would tend to awaken. At any rate, the worst that can very well happen, if a silent meeting fails to help, is that it is *nothing.* It would scarcely seem possible that it should delude anyone into a hollow sense of having been engaged in a religious service. But here I am aware of being near the treacherous ground of idiosyncrasy, and I do not wish to press the point.

Hitherto I have been speaking of our meetings for public worship. But, as Friends love to say, our worship does not begin when we sit down together in our public assemblies, nor end when we leave them. The worship in spirit and in truth is in no way limited by time and place. The same idea of a waiting "in the silence of all flesh" to hear the voice of the Lord speaking within us, characterizes the Friends' private times of worship ; or, as the more cautious expression is, of "religious retirement." Friends are so possessed with the sense of our inability to offer acceptable prayer in our own time and will, that where others speak of family prayers, and hours of prayer or devotion, Friends prefer the expressions, "family reading" and "religious retirement."

And not only in name, but in method, are these times marked with the same peculiar character as our public meetings. In Friends' families of the old-fashioned type (which are more numerous still, I fancy, than many people suspect) the family meeting consists simply of the reading of a portion of Scripture, and then a pause of silence, which may or may not be broken by words of prayer or of testimony. Many Friends formerly (and some, I believe, still feel the same) objected on conscientious grounds to their children's learning to use any form of prayer, even the Lord's.

Prayer. The children shared from the first in the united silence of the family, and could not fail to know what it meant : but in some families it was rarely or never broken by vocal prayer. A silent pause before meals is the Friends' equivalent for "saying grace "— a practice which I own I think has much to recommend it. Here, again, there is, of course, the opportunity for words, should words spontaneously arise to the lips of any of those present.

When we penetrate into the inmost chamber of private worship differences of method can no longer be traced by human eye. It is not possible for any one to judge of the practice of others in this respect ; nay, there seems an impropriety in following individuals into this sacred region, even in thought. Sectarian differences must here be left behind. But for that very reason I may here appeal with the greater fulness of confidence to the sympathy of all who pray, in the attempt, from which I feel it impossible to refrain, to explain the way in which a belief in present inspiration is, as I think, inseparable from belief in the reality and the rightness of prayer.

I trust that I shall not be thought presumptuous for entering upon this subject. There are many qualifications for it which I do not possess. But on matters of common and urgent interest the very absence of distinguishing power or knowledge may give a certain value to the results of actual personal experience, as lessening the distance across which the helping hand has to reach out.

I believe that the permanent effect for good or for

evil of the present shaking and upheaval of thought
amongst us must be mainly determined by its relation
to prayer. No immediate result of the outbreak of free
discussion of all things in heaven and earth during the
last thirty years has been so agonizing to devout persons,
nor so gravely threatens spiritual health, as the paralysis
which in many cases it has seemed to bring upon the
spirit of prayer. We meet daily with open denials of
the reasonableness of prayer—of the possibility of
entering into any real communication with the Divine
being. Few amongst us can have altogether escaped
the paralyzing influence of the flood of unsolved, and
apparently insoluble, moral problems, and at the same
time of new and absorbingly interesting views of
material things, into which this generation has been
plunged. The mere demand on the attention is powerful enough to drain away great part of the mental
power formerly employed in seeking after God.

> " It seems His newer will,
> We should not think of Him at all, but trudge it ;
> And of the world He has assigned us make
> What best we can,"

says A. H. Clough ; and he utters, I am sure, a widely
spread feeling. People's very love of truth seems to
themselves to be enlisted in pursuing the streams which
lead them away from the Fountain of truth. And the
pursuit of scientific truth is assuredly in its place a con-
tribution to our knowledge of God, though made by
workers who may but too easily themselves lose sight
of Him in their engrossing preoccupation with His
works.

But the tendency to put prayer to silence is not merely thus indirect. The one idea which seems at present most forcibly to have grasped the popular imagination, is that of the universal and inexorable dominion of unchanging law. And the inference is not unnatural, "Then it is useless to pray." The result is an awful silence—not of the flesh, indeed, but of the spirit. Men and women have come to feel themselves alone in a new and fearful sense—alone as in the valley of dry bones, with no expectation of any Divine breath to cause them to stand up upon their feet, a united host of living servants of the living God.

I trust that I shall not be suspected of any intention of grappling with the problem of freewill and necessity. I know, at least, enough to be aware that there is at the end of every avenue of human thought an impenetrable mystery. But I also know that the region in which philosophers join issue upon the question of necessity lies far beyond the range of any such practical questions as I am engaged with. I know that the controversy is not decided, and, so far as we can see, does not visibly approach towards a decision ; I know also that no conceivable agreement of philosophers as to the most accurate way of stating facts can alter the facts themselves with which we have to do. I do not hope to express myself with philosophical accuracy ; but I can, and will, speak plainly and truly of my own experience in this matter of prayer.

There was a time when I myself was silenced by the paralyzing influences of which I have spoken—when the heavens seemed as brass, and to ask for anything seemed like flying in the face of one vast foregone conclusion ; as though a moth should dash itself against an iceberg. But I have come to believe that the truth against which I had thus, so to speak, stumbled in the dark, was not that prayer is unreasonable, but that my ideas of prayer were unworthy.

That the will of God is unchangeable (in the sense of absolute self-consistency), is assuredly the very foundation of all reasonable trust in Him, and is recognized by saints and philosophers alike. But does not the imagination easily confound unchangeableness with immovableness? Are not the laws of motion as fixed as those of space? What can be more full of movement than the flames of fire? Yet are they less unchangeable in their nature than a bar of iron? Is it not through a reliance upon the unchangeable properties of material things that we are able to change the whole face of the earth? And should we not remember that the unchangeable order which all things, visible and invisible obey, includes all the mysterious movements of mind, the unknown sources of perpetual "variation," and the most unfathomable of all mysteries, life itself?

It seems to me that when our imagination smites everything with rigidity, it is really playing us a trick. Those who are at all competent to expound the theory of necessity are earnest to show that it in no way contradicts the efficacy of effort in any possible direction. They have need to be earnest about it, for the imagination is but too ready for a pretext to hoist the flag of despair, and the will to throw up the game of life, and to sink into the sleep of apathy.

If we are right in thinking of God as the Fountain of life and thought, the Father of spirits—and to those who deny this it is idle for me to address myself—it can surely not be unreasonable for the spirits He has made to seek to hold communion with Him. What *is* often unreasonable is the nature of our requests, and our idea of the possibility of their being granted. Here it is that I have had to recognize the unworthiness of many of my own thoughts and expressions about prayer, and that I continually meet with what seems to me unfit and inadequate in the language of others. It cannot be an unimportant thing that we should endeavour to sift out what is untenable and unbecoming from our thoughts and words on this subject.

Two things have, as I believe, mainly tended to lower our idea of prayer, until, in minds where it is but a theory, it has been shattered against the hard facts of science. We have narrowed it to the idea of asking for things, and we have thought of it chiefly as a means of getting them.

This is surely a degradation of the idea of prayer, even though the things asked for be what are called "spiritual blessings." The word "prayer" may, it is true, be used in the restricted sense of making requests ; but in that case let it be distinctly understood and kept in the mind that it is but a part—the lowest and least essential part—of worship or communion with God. It is of prayer in the larger sense—not request, but communion—that we may rightly and wisely speak as the very breath of our spiritual life ; as the power by which life is transfigured ; as that to which all things are possible. But this distinction between request and communion is *not* habitually kept in mind by those who write and speak of prayer, nor even by all those who practise it. It seems to me as if many even deeply experienced Christians were using all their energy to encourage and stimulate above all that part of prayer which has surely the most of the merely human and carnal in it, rather than to show forth that nobler part to which this should be but the innocent and natural prelude. If we fall back, as we must perpetually do, upon our Lord's own leading principle of using the human relation of parent and child as the highest and most instructive type of the relation between God and the human spirit, we shall surely feel that the child, in learning to speak to its father and to understand his voice, has far other and larger hopes and purposes than that of getting things from him. The human parent may use the child's innocent and natural wishes as one means of attracting its attention, but would surely be grievously disappointed if the child never looked beyond the advantages to be reaped by the power of speaking to its father—never rose to the perception that intercourse with him was in itself the greatest of human joys, not a mere means to an end.

And in the same sort of sense I feel that, when people insist upon " the efficacy of prayer," they are insisting upon its very lowest use ; and that the concentration of attention upon this lowest use creates a serious stumbling-block, which hinders faith in two ways.

1. It suggests a *test* which is not and cannot be uniformly favourable. Whatever the power of prayer may

be—and words, I believe, must wholly fail to express it—particular requests are certainly not always granted. Our Lord explicitly prepares us for the refusal of blind requests, and our own good sense and our daily experience combine to make it abundantly clear that many requests are, and must always be, refused.

2. And more than this, there is, I believe, nobility enough in every heart capable of real prayer to cause a recoil from the idea of using it only for the purpose of obtaining advantages, be they of what kind they may. I believe, that is, that the modern perplexity about prayer arises not only from a difficulty in imagining God as One who can be influenced by our desires, but largely also from a latent sense that, even if true in fact, this is a very inadequate conception of Him to whom our worship should be addressed, and who must assuredly know better than we do what things we have need of—from a recoil, in short, against the low and coarse and unworthy tone of much that is urged on the other side.

Therefore I think that in the long-run an immeasurable gain will result to faith from modern outspokenness in recognizing the difficulties of this subject. Prayer, if regarded as an attempt to wrest favours from our heavenly Father by dint of mere importunity, is doomed to many disappointments, and stands sorely in need of their purifying discipline. Prayer is not really prayer—that is, it is not true communion with God—till it rises above the region in which wilfulness is possible, to the height of " Not my will, but Thine, be done."

Importunity may, indeed, prevail to win attention from a reluctant or drowsy human ear. Our Lord Himself reminds us of this fact to reprove the faint-heartedness which would allow itself to be discouraged by delay. But the ear of the Father is ever open to our prayers. We cannot think that importunity is needed to rouse His attention. The hindrance when He refuses, or delays to grant, our requests must be of a very different kind. If once we recognize that He hears us always, and that in everything that happens we may hear His voice answering us, we are forced also to recognize that severe discipline is as truly a part of His answer as tender indulgence. Both are welcomed by the childlike heart ; both are part of the language we have patiently to learn to interpret.

But then comes the question, What is there to convince us that we are listened to at all, if the answer is everything equally ? If it is in the whole course of events that we are to look for the answer and that course is as often as not contrary to our prayer, how are we justified in saying that prayer is ever answered ?

It is the answer to this question, What is it that does, in fact, produce a reasonable conviction that we are listened to ? which, I think, involves that theory of inspiration which Friends, more markedly than any other body of Christians, have always avowed and acted upon. But, in trying to reply to it, I wish it to be distinctly borne in mind that I am giving, for what it is worth, the result of my own personal exercises of mind, not undertaking to state recognized

Quaker doctrine.* Difficulties, though probably in essence the same from generation to generation, come before each generation in a fresh form, and need to be freshly met by individual experience.

That which produces a reasonable conviction that prayer is answered must, surely, be the sense of Divine guidance of which I have already spoken in the last chapter. The general grounds for our common belief in God as the Father of spirits are too deep and too wide for me to set forth. As I have already said, I assume such a belief as the groundwork of all that I am attempting to unfold. That which enables each one of us who believe in Him to discern His voice is, as already suggested, a touch as of a hand upon our arm, a dealing with our own spirit and life of so personal and in-

---

* In what follows there is, indeed, no "doctrine" of any kind ; no attempt, I mean, to offer formulated or authorized teaching. I have endeavoured to show how in my own experience the intellectual difficulties with which the subject is surrounded did, when honestly and patiently faced, prove in due time the means of purifying, not of quenching, that true spirit of prayer which is indeed the very breath of our inner life. I trust that none will misunderstand my outspokenness in stating those difficulties. They are, and in these days must be, freely recognized. Unless we who have a witness to bear for the Author of spiritual worship are willing to face them, our witness will fail to reach those who most sorely need it. I am driven once more to appeal to "something more than candour" in my readers for a right interpretation of my struggle to unfold thoughts which tax my powers of utterance to the uttermost, and which yet I dare not withhold.

dividual and significant a nature as that we cannot help feeling that " the finger of God is come unto us."

If this be, indeed, the right direction in which to look for answers to prayer, then the whole subject is withdrawn from the region in which positive proof or disproof are possible. Our interpretation of such individual experiences is that upon which the whole controversy turns, and this must of necessity result from the nature of our previous belief respecting much more general truths. It will always be open to those who disbelieve in God to call His signs " mere coincidences." It is surely not therefore the less reasonable for those who do believe in him to be on the watch for every possible faintest indication of His pleasure. There must be in this, as in all other matters, a preparation of heart and mind before any sign, however eloquent, can take effect upon us. In point of fact we know that the sense of receiving a personal communication from above is not always excited by the granting of a petition. After we have asked and received, no less than when we have asked and not received, we are sometimes inclined to say, " After all, does my prayer make any difference ? would not things have happened just in the same way if I had not prayed ?" This is a question to which, in truth, I believe that we must be content (so far, at least, as regards any particular instance) to remain without an answer. We can never really know what would have happened if we had not prayed.

To say this is, of course, by no means to deny that our prayer has made a real though unknown difference.

It is, on the contrary, almost positively to assert the action of unmeasured and unfathomable influences. We cannot measure the whole results of any action, however insignificant ; but the whole tendency of modern "scientific" thought, and of belief in " necessity," at any rate, goes to show that all things are so interdependent that an action without results is almost inconceivable. Necessitarians, of all people, are bound to admit this. The action of prayer cannot, however, be traced by human eyes, and the longing to know precisely *what* difference our prayer makes to the course of events is, I believe, a longing which can never be gratified in this world.

Yet a power which we cannot precisely measure may make itself continually felt, and the power of prayer is in some lives a matter of perpetually renewed if incommunicable experience. The testimony of those who can thankfully and reverently say that their prayers are answered in a manner that is wonderful in their own eyes, is too familiar and too sacred to all of us to need insisting upon. Its weight is, I believe, strictly speaking immeasurable. But it is in a manner naturally veiled from hasty or external observation, and is, therefore, easily disregarded. When fully considered, it will be found to consist mainly in combinations of circumstances by no means incredible in themselves. It is not the accuracy of the facts recorded by those to whom prayer is a reality, but the explanation of their combination, which is generally in question. If I am right in supposing that we can never trace the precise relation of cause and effect between prayer and the answer, this difficulty—the difficulty, I mean, of exhaustively explaining significant combinations of circumstances—is not surprising. It is the natural result of our being out of our depth.

But although the whole region into which we plunge when we begin to speak of the answer to our prayers is of necessity unfathomable by us, we may with advantage remember that there are some special difficulties besetting any attempt to share with others the experiences which have naturally and rightly most weight with ourselves ; and that by disregarding these difficulties we convert them into stumbling-blocks.

One main difficulty of this kind lies in the factth at the outward events of which we can speak most freely, which we can, as it were, without impropriety call others to witness, must be more or less public in their nature ; such as, e.g., the preservation of lives dear to us, political or national events, favourable changes of weather, and so on—things as to which it is not upon any theory reasonable to suppose that they can be determined with reference only to the wishes or the prayers of any one individual. Even if they went according to my personal wishes and prayers, there would be a manifest impropriety in claiming them as having been thereby brought about. If I pray that the sun may rise to-morrow morning, it does not need much faith to feel sure I shall not be refused, but it would be grossly improper to claim that the event had occurred " in answer to my prayers." When the Prince of Wales recovered from his fever, there were many who would have thought it impious to doubt that his recovery was actually *caused* by the many prayers which were undoubtedly offered on his behalf. Other people were and will remain convinced that he would equally have recovered in any case. Who can attempt to decide between these opinions with any show of authority? Indeed it appears to me that both are presumptuous. Children must often be content to accept their parents' decision without understanding all the motives (if, indeed, we should dare to attribute motives to God) by which it may have been prompted.

In the case of many events (such as battles, weather, and so on) which must necessarily be unfavourable to the wishes of one side and favourable to the other, we know that some prayers must be granted while some are refused. Who will attempt to trace the proportion between request and result? or to treat the influence of prayer in such matters as admitting of either proof or disproof?

But when we come to the circumstances of each individual life, the case is very different. We do not get rid of mystery even here. Our knowledge, even of our own lives, is altogether imperfect and fragmentary; but to pretend to know no more about the ordering of them than we do about the universe would be mere dishonesty. We *can* trace a correspondence between our desires and their accomplishment when it occurs in our own lives, such as it would be mere impertinence to try to trace between, *e.g.*, our desires and the history of a nation. You may call it superstition to say, " I prayed for strength and my request was granted, for strength was given me "; but you cannot accuse me of gross impropriety in thus associating my prayer and the event, as you would if I said, "I prayed that the sun might rise, and my request has been granted." It is within our own personal experience that we must look for the answer which we can rightly appropriate.

But, then, in proportion as the event is brought within the personal sphere of one individual, it is necessarily removed from that of others. Those parts of our personal and separate experience of which we can speak freely are almost necessarily superficial. I do not doubt that even trifles are a part of the Divine language to individuals, but trifles cannot with propriety be appealed to for the purpose of convincing others. Those personal experiences, on the other hand, which are at once deep enough and individual enough to be the fittest subjects of prayer (in the sense of special request) and to be met by responsive "providences" of a peculiarly impressive kind, are almost always such as, for a very different reason, we are unable to mention with much freedom. The whole cogency of the reason which is rightly conclusive to oneself, in short, generally depends upon facts of personal feeling, and upon minute correspondences of events with intricate chains of previous experience, such as human language would fail to transmit, even did a right instinct of modesty not forbid the attempt. We are, therefore, for our share in this universal experience of the people of God, very much shut up—and I think there is in the fact a beautiful fitness—to the individual and separate teaching of life. I believe that we cannot (if it be true) too clearly and unflinchingly make the assertion that our private experience has convinced us of the reality of the Divine response to prayer ; but also, that we cannot be too cautious how we try to utter such experience itself. Simple-minded people, who live much in the practice of prayer, and whose habitual expectation of a Divine response is continually (and to themselves often wonderfully) fulfilled, are often exposed to the snare of making public what should be sacredly kept for themselves alone, or at least shared only with those who " have ears to hear." Much mischief is, I fear, often done by the too free and ready communication, especially in print, of " remarkable answers to prayer "; of incidents which, overpoweringly eloquent as they may well be to those whom they concern, are but as an idle tale to strangers—a tale the telling of which sometimes lends itself but too easily to the mere love of signs and wonders. They also often lay bare the most painful effects of unconscious self-importance—the most glaring tendency to refer everything to oneself as the centre, and to ignore the legitimate share of others in the events referred to. One is almost inclined to say of such stories that, the more wonderful they are, the less edifying they are likely to be.

For it is not in such outward and tangible events as these, not in the things which can be passed from hand to hand like coins, that the real power and soul-subduing influence of a Divine communication is most unmistakably felt. It is the still small voice which overcomes ; the gentle combination of perhaps very ordinary circumstances, which, when combined, acquire the significance of a distinct message. Just as when we see letters brought together and placed under our eyes, which together form a word replying to our thought, we infer that they have been so arranged by some one who knew what was in our minds ; so, to those of us who habitually not only ask but watch for Divine instruction, there occur again and again combinations of events, adjustments even of the minutest details, which produce a quite irresistible sense that the finger of God is pointing the lesson He would have us learn.

It is idle to ask those who never listen whether and how God answers prayer. The very possibility of discerning the answer implies docility and willingness of heart. The High and Holy One that inhabiteth eternity dwells with him who is of an humble and contrite spirit, and such only can learn to know His voice.

To those who in any degree do know His voice, it gradually becomes clear that prayer and its answer are inseparable. The answer is as the answer of the atmosphere to the lungs, of light to the eyes. The humble and contrite heart opens its doors to its Maker, and is filled with His presence. Then, indeed, the light shines within ; then the very breath of our life is breathed into us by the Spirit of God. Inspiration —the inbreathing power from above, by which alone all that is heavenly in us is brought about,—this is the other aspect of worship.

True worship, therefore, implies inspiration. It is the inspired prayer which transfigures life—which is mighty with the might of the Fountain from whence it flows. While we separate worship and inspiration we can never think worthily of either. I do indeed believe that the very desire of our heart is often granted to us in reply to our petition. I do not venture to speak confidently as to the precise relation of cause and effect which may exist between any petition and its fulfilment. There must, I believe, be some such real relation : but to my own mind it often seems more probable and more reverent to suppose, where the correspondence is very marked, that the prayer has been in the nature of a prophetic utterance, of a Divine foreshadowing, than that our wish should have been allowed to become the efficient cause of the Divine action. A prayer which has been answered by the perfect fulfilment of its requests shows, I believe, that the offerer of it was so far under Divine influence ; that his will was to that extent at least in harmony with the Divine will. This is a word of blessed encouragement for the one to whom it comes, which it is not always wise or right to proclaim from the housetop. "Upliftings unto prayer" (to quote one more of the deep words of A. H. Clough) are surely among the sacred things of which we should not lightly lift the veil. I do not think that those who have any true and deep experience of what it is to hold communion, however faltering and intermittent, with our God will be forward to attempt to divest it of its mystery, while yet they must earnestly desire to set forth to others what they have learnt of its power and its blessedness. For the sake of the many who honestly desire to know the truth upon this deepest and most urgent of all common interests, I think that we who

F

have some such experience are bound to seek to clothe it in fit and worthy language.

Let us, therefore, recognize and avow, when occasion serves, that prayer, worship, or communion with God is a larger, deeper, fuller thing than mere asking and having. Let us acknowledge that the simplest and most inarticulate cry for help—the voice of the " infant crying in the night, and with no language but a cry "—is as sure to enter the ear of the Father of spirits as the deepest prayer ever uttered by saint or martyr. Let us remember that, according to the teaching of our Lord Himself, the one voice which is more sure (if degrees of sureness there can be) than any other of being listened to by the good Shepherd, is the voice of the one who has strayed the furthest from the fold, and is the most deeply conscious of being afar off—the voice of the lost sheep over whose first turning towards home the very angels in heaven rejoice with a special joy. But let us never forget that in the homeward path there are heights beyond heights ; that as any spirit is drawn upwards by the Father's love and care, it becomes more and more filled with the light of His countenance, more interpenetrated by that light which shines clearest in the dark places through which every upward-tending spirit must assuredly pass. Let us not forget that the reward of faithfulness in that which is least is the call to enter into that which is greater—deeper and higher and fuller of Divine significance ; that those " influences of the Divine presence " to which it is the essence of true worship to " yield ourselves " must penetrate into the

inmost recesses of our being, and bring every thought
into subjection to the law of Christ—that law of the
Spirit of life, by which all that is of the flesh is
gradually purged away as by a consuming fire—and
that to live in the spirit of prayer is to live more and
more continually and intimately in the presence of
Him before whom the angels veil their faces, and who
is of purer eyes than to behold iniquity. So that it
may well be, or rather it can only be, in fear and in
trembling that this wonderful salvation of entrance into
His presence can be worked out. The prayers which
are owned by Him are not prayers which can be offered
in the will of man, or which can be used as a means of
gratifying the desires of the flesh or of the reason ;
they are the breathings of the spirit struggling to return to Him who gave it, or rejoicing in the light of
His countenance. The spirit which is being made free
from the law of sin and death cannot look backwards
towards the things of earth. Its path is onwards and
upwards, ever " into light," and its breathings are the
vibrations communicated to it from the Source and
Centre of light ; they obey a law as unchangeable as
the laws of light itself, and their function is to destroy
and to consume away the perishing, worn-out raiment
of the spirit, to free it from defilements and hindrances,
and to bring it forth in the fullness of time " into the
glorious liberty of the children of God," the rightful
" inheritance of the saints in light." Surely we may
with reverence say that, in a true and a deep sense,
God Himself is the answer to prayer.

CHAPTER IV.

FREE MINISTRY.

OUR ministry may be said to be free in several distinct senses.

1. It is open to all.
2. Its exercise is not subject to any pre-arrangement.
3. It is not paid.

We believe that the one essential qualification for the office of a minister is the anointing of the Holy Spirit ; and that this anointing is poured out without respect of persons upon men and women, upon old and young, upon learned and unlearned. The gift is, we believe, a purely spiritual one, as much beyond our control as the rain from heaven ; yet as unfailing, as abundant, as necessary to fertility.

Our views of this matter differ from those of other Christians, not in the fact that we recognize the free gift of this holy anointing, not even in the fact that we repudiate the idea of its being purchasable by money, but in the fact that our idea of ministry refers exclusively to the offering of spontaneous spiritual ministrations. All would surely agree that it is impossible for any one to offer acceptable prayer, or to sow

in other hearts the living seed of the kingdom, without
a distinct gift from above. It is obvious that we cannot
give what we have not received. It is also surely undeniable that what we have freely received we should
freely give ; that the gift of God cannot be bought for
money, nor restricted in its exercise to humanly prepared
channels. No one who believes in the reality of the gift
of "prophecy"—of speaking, that is, from the immediate
promptings of the Spirit of Truth—would dare to seek
either to purchase or to restrain such utterances.
"Where the Spirit of the Lord is, there is liberty."
Our doctrine of a free ministry, of course, supposes
a real belief in the continual inbreathing of that Divine
Spirit, giving both light and utterance through His own
chosen vessels for the help of all. It also goes a step
further, and regards such spiritual ministrations as all-
sufficient. Here is the real point of divergence between
us and our fellow-Christians. The vast majority of
them regard something more than these purely spiritual
ministrations as essential to a full allegiance to our
common Lord.

Other Christian bodies have from very early times
recognized a distinction between clergy and laity, and
have regarded at least two sacraments as having been
instituted by Christ Himself and as being in some
sense or other "necessary to salvation" ; and the
greater number, or at any rate the largest, of these
bodies have habitually adopted the use of liturgical
forms of public worship.

At the root of our abstinence from all these generally
accepted practices, there lies the one conviction of the

all-sufficiency of individual and immediate communication with the Father of our spirits ; and a profound belief that by His coming in the flesh our Lord Jesus Christ did, in fact, open a new and living way of access to God, which superseded and blotted out the former dispensation of rites and ceremonies, investing all believers with the function of "kings and priests" (calling them that is, both to exercise dominion and to offer acceptable sacrifices in His name), and enabling them to show forth the nature and results of that worship in spirit and in truth, which was no longer to be in any sense confined to temples made with hands, and of that kingdom which is "not meat and drink, but righteousness and peace and joy in the Holy Ghost."

It was a bold thing indeed for the early Friends to break loose at once from the whole ecclesiastical system, with its venerable and long established claim to be the divinely ordained channel of spiritual nutriment. In doing so, they no doubt took up an attitude of hostility towards the " hireling priests," and their "steeple-houses " and "so-called ordinances," which, however comparatively intelligible it may have been at the time, was yet not only highly obnoxious, but would even seem to have led them into some degree of injustice.

After sixty or seventy years of severe persecution, however, borne with extraordinary patience as well as constancy, their right to carry out their own manner of worship was fully allowed ; and by a strange result of changes partly within the Society itself and partly in the surrounding mental atmosphere, Friends, from being regarded as peculiarly pestilent heretics, came to be looked on as the most harmless and least obnoxious of Nonconformists. I believe, however, that this can be the case only as long as we are content to acquiesce in a purely passive and dwindling state. Any attempt to promulgate our peculiar views must necessarily give offence. We may, perhaps, no longer think it a duty to denounce the institution of a separate clergy and the observance of "so-called ordinances," as positively unlawful or sinful. But to say plainly that we consider them as superfluous, requires hardly less boldness, and is scarcely likely to be more palatable. The fact, however, cannot be disguised ; and in spite of the pain which, in these days of free and lively interchange of sympathy, is involved in taking up any clear ground of separation, no true Friend would desire in the slightest degree to disguise or to veil our ancient testimony against outward observances and their accompanying institution of a paid ministry.

It is, however, a great help in doing so to be able to point to the very remarkable fact of the existence during more than two centuries of a body of people whose lives bear abundant witness to the reality of their Christian profession, amongst whom these "ordinances" have been altogether disused.

For my own part, I would rather leave that fact to speak for itself than attempt to trace all the inferences which may, I think, fairly be drawn from it. Yet the question whether the clerical and sacramental system is indeed an essential part of Christianity, or a human accretion, is too profoundly important to the future of Christianity itself to be lightly passed over. Are there not many, in these days especially, who would willingly listen to the Christianity of Christ Himself, could they but find it disentangled from the enormously "developed" Christianity of the dominant Churches?

I am far from venturing to claim that the Society of Friends does actually exhibit a perfect living instance of what has been called "primitive Christianity revived," but I do believe its ideal to be the true, and the only true one; that of a Church, or "gathered people," living with the one object of obeying the teaching of Christ Himself to the very uttermost—His own teaching, not that of those who have spoken in His name, even though they be apostles, except in so far as they speak in accordance with it. To *live* the Sermon on the Mount, and the rest of the gospel teaching, and in all things to listen for the living voice of the good Shepherd, watching constantly that no human tradition divert our attention from it,—this is our acknowledged aim and bond of union as a Society. Our conviction of its sufficiency is the ground of our existence as a separate body.

We believe that neither the division of Christian people into clergy and laity, nor the use of sacramental ceremonies, were enjoined by Christ Himself. It is clear that both these practices quickly arose amongst the early Christians; but remembering that the early Christians were but fallible human beings like ourselves, and that they were undeniably far from clear what rites and ceremonies were to be observed, we do not feel that their practice is to be our guide.

The institution of a separate clergy and that of the sacraments form, of course, essentially one system. The early Friends went to the root of the matter when they abandoned at once the whole of what they called "mountain and Jerusalem worship," as opposed to the worship in Spirit and in truth, which is not limited to any time or place.

I have not the slightest intention of taking upon myself the attempt to show that they were right in doing so. The grounds of their action are fully set forth and defended with undeniable vigour and ability by Robert Barclay in his famous "Apology." My humbler endeavour will be to describe the perplexities which prepared my own mind thankfully to accept what to myself appears to be a thoroughly satisfactory disentanglement of essential Christianity from whatever can be honestly regarded as unintelligible, and unworthy of its lofty and spiritual character.

I must own at the outset that I have never been able clearly to understand the grounds upon which the "ordinances" in question are regarded as essential parts of Christianity, nor have I ever found it possible to arrive at a thoroughly satisfactory explanation of their precise (supposed) effects. I am, of course, not ignorant of the general nature of those grounds or supposed results. But a broad space of obscurity seems to separate the actual transactions out of which the "ordinances" arose from the earliest known records of the institutions themselves; and it is notorious that theologians differ very widely in their views of the spiritual results produced either by ordination or by a due participation in the sacraments, and also of the conditions necessary to their "validity."

It is here that the practical pinch of the system is felt. Were the matter one of purely speculative interest, how gladly would I and other unlearned people have left it in the hands of those better qualified to deal with it! But it is a question of urgent practical importance, which, as regards at least one of the sacraments, no devout person can escape. Every adult member of the Church of England (every one, that is, who is so in a religious sense) is confronted with a solemn challenge to do, or to leave undone at his peril, an act involving vast and mysterious consequences for good or for evil to his spiritual welfare. No middle course is possible, and the Church Prayer-book promises no safety either in its performance or omission. To "partake unworthily" is represented as involving vague and awful dangers—dangers possibly, though not clearly, greater than those which would be incurred by omitting an act "generally necessary to salvation." But how to be sure of partaking worthily? "A true penitent heart and lively faith . . . a lively and steadfast faith in Christ our Saviour . . . and perfect charity with all men,"—if these are the necessary *preparations* for being "meet partakers of these holy mysteries," failing in which we do but "eat and drink our own damnation" by venturing to partake of them, is it any wonder if the troubled heart is held in a state of continual uneasiness, and shrinks almost equally from the act and from its omission?

Such, at least, was my own painful and long-continued

experience. The injunction to "examine one's self" as a safeguard against unworthy participation did but increase the perplexity and distress. For how can self-examination fail to increase the sense of unworthiness? and how is it possible for any one to imagine himself competent to be judge in his own case?

I do not forget that the Prayerbook suggests (not to say prescribes) a refuge from such perplexities in an application to "some discreet and learned minister of God's Word" for "absolution, and ghostly council and advice." I quite recognise the consistency of this suggestion, which seems to me to confirm the obvious remark already made, that the sacerdotal and sacramental system hangs together, and must be adopted or rejected as a whole. In my own case Protestantism was too strong to allow of my accepting this legitimate corollary of the Church of England doctrine respecting the Lord's Supper. To have recourse to confession and absolution was an impossibility to me, as I believe it to be even yet to the great majority of Englishwomen, and as it is assuredly likely always to be to Englishmen. But I doubt whether any satisfactory resting-place short of it is to be found for those who fully adopt the Anglican view of sacraments.

I do not mean to represent the perplexities and scruples I have spoken of as having constituted the whole of my experience in this matter, or to say that I was quite unable to meet them in a manner more or less provisionally satisfactory to myself. It is true that out of perplexities and scruples sprang doubts and questionings (with which, indeed, the very air I breathed was thick), so that during the twenty years in which I was a regular communicant in the Church of England, I was never able to feel that my own practice was based upon thoroughly clear and solid ground of ascertained truth. Yet in spite of, or rather alongside of, all scruples and questionings as to the real intention of our Lord—if, indeed, he had any intention at all— with regard to any special commemoration of His death by the use of bread and wine, I did earnestly, through- out those years, according to the measure of my ability, endeavour to solve the problem in practice—to make the act of outward "communion" a real occasion of renewed self-dedication, and of inward and spiritual feeding on the bread of life. Such times were, indeed, often occasions of deep spiritual blessing ; but I never could discern that they were so in any other sense than that in which every real act of prayer, of penitence, of self-dedication, of thanksgiving must necessarily be so. The whole blessing appeared to me to be of a spiritual kind, and due to spiritual causes. The connection between the use of bread and wine and these spiritual sources of blessing never became clear to me. The more profound the blessedness of communion with Christ and with His people, the less conceivable did it seem that it should depend upon the official per- formance of an elaborate rite.

The Bible, to which in this Protestant country we are always referred for the solution of the difficulties as to which Catholics consult their priests, appeared to me to afford no help whatever in defining the conditions necessary to a right participation, nor in directing one's choice between the various sacramental theories to be met with in our days. All schools of theology equally appeal to it, and it is obvious that a book cannot decide between rival interpretations of itself. It did, however, distinctly help me towards the conclusion that there might be no need to choose between these various theories at all. To my unassisted reason it appeared that the effect of comparing any, even the mildest, modern eucharistic theory with the accounts to be found in the New Testament of our Lord's parting supper with His disciples, was chiefly to show that a vast and unexplained addition to, or at the least development of, the original idea had taken place since these accounts were written. The whole form of words used in the Communion Service seems to me to convey meanings almost immeasurably different from anything which I could myself have extracted from the one brief expression, " Do this in remembrance of Me." Left to myself and to Scripture, the Gospel narratives would never have suggested the idea of any intention to institute a ceremony at all, far less to invest its observance with possibilities so awful both for good and for evil, not only in case of omission, but even in case of inadequate observance. To my own mind, the narratives of the Last Supper in Matthew and Mark, which contain no allusion to any possible repetition of the feast, appeared quite as complete, quite as significant, as that of Luke, which gives the addition, " Do this in remembrance of Me." The allusions in the Epistle to the Corinthians to some

disorderly practices in that Church certainly make it
clear that they had adopted a practice of meeting to
" show the Lord's death till He come " by eating
bread and drinking wine ; and the apostle's reference
to a Divine communication to himself of the circumstances of the Last Supper certainly seems to show
that he believed them to have sufficient ground for
doing so ; but, on the other hand, the words which he
there ascribes to Christ, " Do this, *as oft as ye drink
it*, in remembrance of me," have always seemed to me
to be distinctly incompatible with the idea of a command to eat bread and drink wine *in order* to com-
memorate His death, and would rather suggest a
reverent remembrance of Him on all social occasions,
and perhaps especially when meeting for the Passover
or any other religious feasts.   I was thus fully ripe
for the view so vigorously put forth in Barclay's
" Apology," * as held by Friends.

I have allowed my thoughts to fall into a somewhat
autobiographical form, because the appearance of
egotism seems to be preferable to the real presumption
of going beyond one's knowledge, and also because I
am anxious to show how unavoidably (and at the
same time, I believe, innocently) one may become
entangled in questions too deep and too perplexing for
ordinary minds, in the mere honest endeavour to obey
at once the teaching of Jesus Christ and of the Church.

To myself it was the greatest relief, at a time when I
had thus been driven to choose between obedience to

---

* " Apology," Prop. xiii.

my own conscience on the one hand, and outward communion with my fellow-Christians on the other, and
when I had for two years, with pain and grief,
excommunicated myself accordingly—it was at that
moment the greatest relief to find a body of Christians
who held the simple, and, to my mind, the one worthy
view of Christianity, as a dispensation entirely spiritual
in its nature; a state of enlightment and true
worship in which forms and shadows had passed away
and the substance alone was to be laboured for. It was
in the quiet meetings already described that I myself
first learnt the full meaning of the words, "baptizing
into the Name . . . and the communion of the
body of Christ." The outward observances by which
these "holy mysteries" are typified in the devotions
of other bodies had been to me rather a hindrance
than a help. I cannot help suspecting that they are so
to many.

For if not a help, they must be a hindrance. It
may, to people in some stages of education, or in some
countries, be a natural and real way of receiving or
expressing truth, to perform ceremonial acts. I cannot
think that it is the spontaneous language of intelligent
devotion in our own time and country. To my own
mind the great crowning lesson imparted by our
Divine Master, in the solemn farewell hours of His
last evening with His disciples, is lowered and eclipsed
when considered as the institution of a ceremony, and
shines out again in its fulness of majestic pathos, when
regarded as an embodied or acted parable. His repeated
warnings to His disciples against their inveterate

tendency to take His word literally, and to interpret
them as referring to the meat that perishes instead of
as being spirit and life, sound in one's ears when one
feels oppressed by what (forgive me the irrepressible
truth) to some of us seems the unintelligent practice of
continually repeating a form used by Christ once for all
to show forth the central truth of His life-giving life on
earth.

It is the fear that, in wrapping the "words of eternal
life" in a garment of superstitious usage, they are being
inevitably buried out of the reach of those who need
them the most, which prompts me to speak thus boldly.
Whatever lowers our religion to a matter of outward
observance, whatever seems to give to unreasoning
participation in outward acts a place on the same level
with that inward continuance in the Word of Christ
which makes His disciples free, is surely a human and
a grievous barrier in the homeward path which He
came to open to all.

Those who feel as we do about the meaning of our
Lord on the occasion of His last supper with His
disciples, will naturally incline to take a similar view
of His meaning in the few references made by Him to
the subject of baptism. The word is obviously used in
the New Testament in several different senses. If we
believe (as is at least suggested by the words of the
Apostle Paul) that there is but "one baptism," we must
surely suppose it to be that baptism "with the Holy
Ghost and with fire" which John foretold as the office
of Him for whom he himself, with his "baptism with
water," was preparing the way;—He who was to

increase as John decreased, and who said of Himself, after He had "fulfilled all righteousness" by submitting to John's baptism, that He had yet " a baptism to be baptized with "—assuredly not an outward one.

With the observance of rites and ceremonies, the need for a separate priesthood passes away. It is, I believe, undisputed that the only Christian priesthood spoken of in the New Testament is that " royal priest- hood " which is the high calling of all believers ; the calling to offer themselves as living sacrifices, holy, acceptable to God.

It appears to us that this priestly office of all believers is greatly obscured, and the sense of religious responsi- bility weakened, by the delegation to a separate and official class of persons of the function of conducting the devotions of the congregation. The exclusive employment of one man as spokesman for the whole congregation must of necessity quench in others any impulse to offer vocal ministrations, at any rate during the time of public worship : and in regard to daily life, the idea of a "cure of souls" seems equally inconsistent with the Quaker idea of " watching over one another for good," as being a duty resting more or less on all the members of a meeting.

There are, of course, many other Church offices besides the essentially priestly one of offering the sacrifice of praise and thanksgiving which are fulfilled, and often nobly fulfilled, by the Clergy of the Church of England. These other offices, such as teaching, visiting the sick, attending to the relief of the poor, etc., are surely in no way inseparable, though they are popularly undistinguished, from that claim to the priesthood against which Friends have always protested. It may be an open question whether all the civilizing, softening, philanthropic, and beneficent influences exercised by the clergy could be brought to bear with equal effect upon the population, especially of country districts, if the idea of an essential distinction between them and the laity were suddenly obliterated. The question, what would be the practical result of such an obliteration, or, in other words, of the adoption of Friends' principle of a free ministry, is at any rate scarcely within the visible horizon. It would certainly be impossible to any candid person in these days to speak without respect and admiration of the clergy generally, and without deep reverence of many amongst them. The days are long past when such phrases as a "hireling ministry" could have been indiscriminately used concerning a body of men whose lives are in innumerable instances so visibly and nobly disinterested. It is an obvious, though too common mistake, to confound the conditions of any service with the motives from which it is undertaken. But it is nevertheless a very grave question, what effect the fact that ordination to the clerical office opens to any young man of ordinary abilities and respectability the gates of an honourable profession, by which he may lawfully earn his bread and maintain a family, is likely to have upon the spiritual character of the ministerial office. Surely the Quaker principle that no spiritual ministrations should ever be subject to payment is at least one that must commend itself as ideally the highest. It may, however, very naturally be asked whether in practice it admits of a sufficient provision being made for the instruction and edification of congregations.

And here there is, of course, a deep-seated divergence of feeling and thought at the bottom of the difference in practice between Friends and other Christian bodies. We Friends believe that it is not necessary that each congregation should be placed under the spiritual care of a pastor. We believe that it is the right and the duty of each individual Christian to approach the Divine presence in his own way—to sit under the immediate teaching of Christ Himself, and to be ready to take his share, if at any time called upon by the one Head of the Church, in offering prayer, praise, thanksgiving, or exhortation, for the help, comfort, and edification of all. Should no vocal services be offered in any meeting, we do not therefore feel that it has failed of its effect as an occasion of united worship.

Some small meetings are frequently, if not habitually, held entirely in silence : in all our meetings, there is some space left for that worship which is beyond words. The responsibility for the lively and healthy state of each meeting is, or should be, felt to rest upon all its members, both collectively and individually.

It is obvious that a ministry so jealously guarded as ours from all external pressure can be kept in vigorous exercise only as the result of a deep and widely diffused religious experience. Serious, though by no means insuperable, difficulties do undoubtedly arise in the practical application of this fundamental principle of our Society. Our faithfulness to it is being severely tested by modern conditions; and upon that faithfulness our very life as a Society must, I believe, depend. There is in the comparatively aggressive attitude we have assumed of late years, as well as in the great pressure upon time and strength exerted by modern activities of all kinds, a constant temptation to adopt methods less pure, less severely disinterested, than those to which we are pledged by all our traditions. Unless we have faith and patience enough to maintain the freedom of our ministry even at the cost of some sacrifice of popularity, I believe that our light must inevitably be extinguished just when it is most urgently needed.*

The admission of the ministry of women seems naturally to flow from the disuse of all but spontaneous spiritual ministrations. For such ministrations experience shows women to be often eminently qualified.

The whole of the Quaker view of ministry depends upon the frank disregard of outward and visible signs in favour of the inward and spiritual grace. To make both essential, or each essential to the other, seems necessarily to land one in impenetrable intricacies, if not in a vicious circle. If one of the two alone is essential, there can of course be no question which it is. Whether inward and spiritual graces, in other words, holiness, can flourish without the use of outward observances, must ultimately be a question of experience and observation. "By their fruits ye shall know them." It might perhaps be

---

* See Appendix, Note B, for a short account of the "Home Mission Committee."

difficult for one born and bred in the Society to appeal explicitly to this test. But having entered it within the last few years, I may perhaps without impropriety say that Friends need surely not shrink from the inquiry whether the practical standard of holiness amongst their members is on a level with that of other Christians. If it be so—if love, joy, peace, long-suffering, gentleness, goodness, faith, meekness, and temperance be not lacking amongst us—surely we may well ask, Wherein does our free ministry fail of its due effect?

" It fails," some would no doubt reply, " not in the quality, but in the quantity of its results. However excellent the results in the life and conversation of Friends individually, they are not a growing body, and therefore not a healthy branch of the Church at large." I shall deal elsewhere with the subject of our long dwindling in former times, and our present slow increase in numbers. I will content myself here with the obvious reply that the numerical increase or decrease of a denomination can never afford a satisfactory test of the spiritual fruitfulness of its ministry ; mere numbers being always affected by many other causes, some of which have but little connection with spiritual health. It even gives but a very doubtful measure of the mere numbers to whom the influence of the preaching in question may extend. It must, no doubt, be admitted that the personal and the numerical tests are apt to yield conflicting results ; that the purest form of religion is rarely the most popular, though it is likely to have the most lasting, and, in the end, the most widely spread influence. But if purity and popularity are in any sense incompatible, can we hesitate as to the direction towards which we should lean ?*

I have said that our corner-stone and foundation is our belief that God does indeed communicate with each one of the spirits He has made in a direct and living inbreathing of some measure of the breath of His own life. That belief is not peculiar to us. What is peculiar to us is our testimony to the freedom and sufficiency of this immediate Divine communication to each one. The ground of our existence as a separate body is our witness to the independence of the true gospel ministry of all forms and ceremonies, and of all humanly imposed limitations and conditions. We desire to guard this supreme function of the human spirit from all disturbing influences as jealously as the mariner guards his compass from anything which might

---

* I believe, as I have already said, that few people outside the Society are aware of the extent to which the practice is still continued of Friends who feel themselves called to the ministry travelling, as we say, " in the service of truth," or "under a sense of religious concern," not only from place to place in England, but also all over the world. A remarkable variety of "services" are in this way spontaneously undertaken, and carried out, sometimes quite alone, sometimes with the help of one or more Friends "liberated" to accompany the minister. And those small meetings where there is but little vocal ministry are objects of special care and concern to the larger meetings of which they form a part ; and many Friends make a practice of visiting them from time to time.

There was also a special service to which ministering Friends formerly often felt themselves called, and which, though much

deflect the needle from the pole : and for the same
reason—that we believe the direct influence of the
Divine Mind upon our own to be our one unerring
Guide in the voyage of life, and that the faculty by
which we discern it is but too easily drawn aside by
human influences. There is, surely, a very deep significance and value in the Protestant instinct of independence in this deepest region. The Quaker tradition of
" non-resistance " has attracted a degree of popular
attention which is, I think, out of all proportion to that
bestowed on the profound and stubborn independence
of Quakerism—its resolute vindication of each man's
individual responsibility to his Maker, and to Him
alone. The supreme value assigned by Friends to consistency of conduct—to strict veracity and integrity,
and other plain moral duties—has, I believe, an
intimate connection with their abandonment of all
reliance upon outward observances, or official support
and absolution. " The answer of a good conscience "

---

disused of late years, is not altogether extinct—that of paying
" religious visits to families " in particular districts ; or, in other
words, of holding meetings for worship and mutual edification
from house to house—generally, but not invariably, amongst our
own members only. These visits are occasions specially adapted
and felt suitable for the exercise of that peculiar gift of " speaking
to the condition of " individuals which some Friends (especially
in former times) seem to have possessed in a remarkable degree.
I believe them to have been of deep value when rightly conducted
by the few possessing a real qualification for such delicate and at
times searching services, but perhaps peculiarly liable to degenerate
into what was neither edifying nor acceptable.

comes into prominence when all extraneous means of purification are discarded. And when outward ordination is seen to be insufficient to enable any one effectually to minister to the deep needs of a troubled spirit, then that ministry which is truly the outcome of the fiery "baptisms" of Divinely appointed discipline assumes its true dignity in our eyes as the only real qualification for reaching the witness in other hearts.

I doubt whether any other Protestant sect recognizes the preciousness of the discipline of suffering as it is recognized by Friends. That it is only through deep experience, both of inward exercises and of outward sorrows, that any one can become fully qualified to hold forth the Word of life to others, is signified by the familiar Quaker expression, "a deeply baptised minister." So strongly have some Friends felt this necessity that they have come to distrust, if not to condemn, whatever appears to them "superficial" or easily produced in ministry. A holy awe, deepening at times, I believe, into even too anxious a restraint, has ever surrounded the exercise of our emphatically "free" ministry—free from all human and outward moulding, precisely in order that it may be the more sacredly reserved to the Divine and inward moulding and restraining as well as impelling power.

The danger of our profoundly "inward" ideal is, of course, in its liability to generate scruples, and a degree of morbid introspectiveness, especially in the exercise of this particular gift. Recognizing fully the deep truth that many "baptisms" have to be passed through by those to whom the priceless gift of ministry is entrusted, and that peculiar trials are apt to precede every special replenishing of the sacred vessel, Friends have sometimes gone on to hold it almost a profanation to speak in meetings for worship except as the immediate result of some such painful exercises. It is easy to see the danger of any such limitation of the manner in which the Divine pleasure may be intimated to individuals. It seems both probable and agreeable to experience that a truly spiritual ministry should vary greatly both in its form and in its degree of depth, in various minds. There is obviously a childlike as well as profound utterance of prayer and praise, and surely of "testimony" or "prophecy" also. But to recognize this diversity is not in the slightest degree to lower our idea of the indispensableness of a Divine warrant for utterance. The scrupulous jealousy which would limit all ministry to one type is a very different thing from that spirit of holy fear which must in this matter, above all, be the beginning of wisdom. I think that those who are the most ready to accept with reverence whatever is offered in simple obedience, the most desirous themselves to learn simply to obey, will also be the first to feel that no one should venture to break the silence in which inward prayer may be arising from other hearts except under the influence (to use the time-honoured Quaker expression) of "a fresh anointing from above." The nearest approach to a description of what we hold to be a right ministry would seem to be—words spoken during, and arising from, actual communion with God.

CHAPTER V.

SPECIAL TESTIMONIES.

THERE are certain points of Christian practice upon which we have been accustomed to lay a degree of stress amounting to peculiarity, although our "testimony" in regard to them does not involve any opposition to the beliefs of other Christian bodies, as does that which we have just been considering respecting the freedom of the ministry and disuse of ordinances. The idea of "testimony," or practical witness-bearing to a stricter obedience to the teaching of Jesus Christ than is thought necessary by the mass of those who are called by His name, has been strongly impressed upon Friends from the very outset, and the persecutions which it brought upon them did but burn it irrevocably into the Quaker mind.

The preaching of the early Friends was, above all things, a preaching of righteousness. I think I cannot be wrong in saying that a greater value has from the first been attached by Friends to practice, as compared with doctrine, than is the case with most other Christian bodies. Obedience to the light which convinces of sin was the sum and substance of George Fox's preaching, and through his epistles and other writings there runs a vigorously practical tone which seems to have been responded to with equal vigour by those whom he addressed.

The early Friends certainly did, as a rule, wonderfully practice what they preached ; and their character for integrity was very quickly, and has been permanently, recognized. It seems to myself inevitable that the appeal to the witness in each heart should reach deeper, and bring forth correspondingly better fruit of obedience, when disentangled from all reliance on external passports to Divine favour. Not only the idea of any possible "efficacy of sacraments" as apart from righteousness of life, but also the idea of "substitution " as distinguished from actual experience of the transforming power of the righteousness of Christ, were vigorously rejected by the early Friends ; and in this insistence upon the identity of righteousness with salvation lay, as I believe, the main secret of their strength. At any rate, there has been a remarkably steady endeavour to maintain a high and definite standard of Christian morality, partly by means of the discipline of the Society, partly by family tradition, discipline, and example. Certain "testimonies," *i.e.,* practices conscientiously adopted, inculcated, and watched over, have been handed down from generation to generation with a jealous care which, though sometimes overshooting its mark and tending to produce reaction, has nevertheless moulded the very inmost springs of action, and produced and maintained a distinct and somewhat singular type of Christian character.

The essence of Quaker "testimony" is a practical witness-bearing—a lifting up in practice of the highest possible standard of uncompromising obedience to the teaching of Jesus Christ, both as recorded in the Gospels and as inwardly experienced as the Light—the Spirit of Truth. Friends have, as a matter of fact, felt certain things to be inconsistent with this teaching which, by the great body of those who profess and call themselves Christians, are not regarded as being so. They have attacked these things not so much in words as by enjoining and observing a strict abstinence from them at any cost, in a spirit not unlike that of the Rechabites of old. The original Quaker idea was before all things to have " clean hands " ; to stand clear of evil in one's own person, but to abstain in silence unless specially called to speak.*

It is, of course, impossible to abstain on conscientious grounds from what is freely practised by others without giving some offence. Any singularity of this kind will inevitably be understood as casting some shade of disapprobation, if not of actual blame, on the common practice. I do not see how we can avoid this offence unless we are content to sink to the level of least enlightenment. We must, I believe, nerve ourselves to endure the giving of it, remembering that the disciple is not above his Master, and that there was a

---

* For a short account of the manner in which, before the end of the eighteenth century, the Society in America freed itself from all complicity with slavery, as illustrating the working both of our principles, and of our organization, see Appendix, Note C.

time when our Master Himself had "no honour in His own country." If they have heard His word, they will hear ours also. Meanwhile we may take heart from the knowledge that conduct destined to have permanent influence must often displease for a time.

The early Friends, or "children of light," as they sometimes called themselves, seem to have been drawn together in a kind of spontaneous unanimity on the main points in which their view of Christian duty transcended that of those about them. The Yearly Meeting, which was not constituted till 1672 (or twenty-four years from the date of George Fox's beginning to preach), finding the "testimonies" against war, oaths, and superfluities already in full practice, expressly recognized them as belonging to "our Christian profession," and directed inquiry as to the faithfulness of Friends in maintaining them to be made in certain queries addressed from time to time to all the subordinate meetings.

The practice of addressing such queries to the subordinate meetings is maintained to this day, although the queries themselves have from time to time been altered, and of late years the greater number of them are directed to be seriously considered, but not answered. This change in our practice has probably not been without a balance of advantage and disadvantage. The system of requiring answers to the queries, was, in truth, a very powerful engine of discipline, for they were considered and answered with scrupulous care and precision, and, in case of an unfavourable report. individuals who were regarded as failing to maintain the testimonies of the Society were liable to be "put under dealing," and, in case of obduracy, to eventual disownment. This ultimate penalty of disobedience was in former times inflicted for much slighter causes than would at the present day render any one liable to it.*

It seems to me that there is a serious danger inherent in the very nature of collective testimonies, especially those which imply the lifting up of a standard of exceptional severity and purity, lest that which is in some, perhaps even in the majority, sincere and spontaneous should be adopted at second hand, and without personal warrant, by others, and should thus become a mere hollow profession. For this reason I am thankful that a much greater degree of freedom is now allowed to our members in all matters as to which there is room for a conscientious difference of opinion. Our strength seems to me to depend largely upon our consistency in appealing to the gospel rather than to the law—in trusting to the purifying power of an indwelling, informing Spirit, rather than to any external frame work

---

* The expression "put under dealing" describes the prescribed preliminary to disownment. When an overseer, having found private remonstrance unavailing, is obliged to bring a case of wrong-doing before the Monthly Meeting, that Meeting appoints one or two Friends to visit and "deal with" the offender, in the way of exhortation and counsel, with a view to induce him to acknowledge and condemn or "disown" his own fault, and thus to avert the penalty of the Society's disownment of himself.

of regulations. To do anything which can stimulate the profession of more or higher enlightenment than is actually possessed, is indeed a signal and a grievous departure from our own avowed principles; and I believe that no surer method could be devised for bringing our Society into disrepute and decay than the attempt to require a pre-arranged uniformity with regard to those special testimonies which imply special enlightenment.

The loftier and more delicate the ideal, the greater the risk of formulating and attempting to impose it. It seems to me that our wisdom is to insist more and more boldly upon obedience to the broad plain laws of duty which all Christians recognise as laid down for us by those recorded words of our Master Himself, which are our one supreme standard; and at the same time to leave more and more scope for the working out in detail of all the lovely and harmonious yet varying results of individual faithfulness to the promptings of His Spirit in each heart. Any distinct breach of the moral law, any falling below that standard of "peaceable innocent life" which is acknowledged by all as the test of the reality of light within, may and should surely be made a matter of Church discipline—a matter, that is, in which brethren should watch over one another for good, and obedience to which must be a condition of sound fellowship. But when discipline attempts the regulation of details whose whole significance and value depend upon their being prompted by conscience, under the living and ever-present guidance of the light, then surely the human is intruding upon the province of the Divine, and we are checking and hampering and weakening that very moulding from within which it is our chief object as a Society to watch for and to yield to in all things.

But while all attempts at collective self-discipline must involve a danger of hollowness, which means weakness, if not actual insincerity, it is to be remembered, on the other hand, that there is in association not only a well-known source of strength, but a very valuable shelter; a protection to right instincts of modesty. In maintaining any exceptionally high standard of action, especially in matters of detail, there is a real safety as well as comfort in united action. While we are treading in the steps of our honoured predecessors, however freely we may have chosen our path, we are not tempted to claim that we discovered it; nor need we anxiously vindicate it as though it were but the prompting of some individual scruple or preference. In the practical results of the collective exercises of a considerable body of fellow-disciples, we do, I believe, in fact find, as we might reasonably expect to find, a peculiar purity and propriety. It is not difficult to justify the wisdom by which our special testimonies have been worked out, though it is easy also to see the mischief of too rigid an enforcement of them.

Our Society, like the United Kingdom, enjoys the elasticity resulting from the absence of any written constitution, and the precise working of its discipline is by no means easily traced. Its "testimonies," though clearly recognized and notorious, are not formulated or

defended in any authoritative document, The "Book
of Discipline" consists, as I have said, of extracts from
"Epistles" and "Advices" circulated from time to
time by the Yearly Meeting. These are in the nature of
brotherly exhortations, which assume our principles as
undisputed; and though carefully worded, they do
not deal in definitions and arguments. Our testimonies
are, in fact, to a degree which is, I think, hardly understood outside the Society, the result of individual
and spontaneous obedience to the bidding of individual
conscience, and to the guiding of the Divine light shining
in each heart, rather than of conformity to rules enforced
or even precisely laid down by any human authority.
They are collective, but unformulated; subjects for
discipline, yet not prescribed or regulated; familiar
and even notorious peculiarities, yet varying indefinitely
in the degree in which they are maintained by individuals.

The traditional reverence for individual conscience
is still so strong that the precise nature of the obstacle
felt by Friends to any particular course of conduct is
apt to be shrouded in some degree of mystery. The
phraseology of the Society, which is almost a separate
language, vividly conveys this sense of an insuperable
but (to outsiders) mysterious restraint. "Truth
requires" that certain things should be done or left
undone. A Friend "feels a stop in his mind," or "is
not easy to proceed with" some undertaking. Such and
such a thing "appears" (to John Woolman, for
instance) "to be distinguishable from pure wisdom."

There are, as is well known, individual Friends who

have abundantly argued, on general grounds, the moral questions involved in our "testimonies." Friends have never been wanting in pugnacity, whatever their scruples as to the use of "carnal weapons" or of violent language. But yet their practice has in the main been felt out rather than thought out; their testimonies are instances of problems solved by going forward rather than of theories built up through any speculative process; and in regard to each one of them every true Friend feels that to his own Master he stands or falls. and that there is but one Example to which he ought to look, and one Guide whom he desires to obey. As in regard to our public ministry, so in the lesser matters of everyday life and practice, we jealously guard our individual liberty from human interference in order that it may be the more unreservedly subjected to all Divine influences.

And not only do we guard our own liberty—we refrain from attempting to limit that of others. If our conscientious abstinence from certain practices is inevitably understood as in some sense casting a shadow of reproach or blame upon those practices, we yet are careful to abstain from condemning those who are acting in obedience to their own measure of light. I believe we must with boldness and humility acknowledge that such practical witness-bearing as we believe ourselves called to, implies that we are as "a city set on a hill." We do not attempt to lay down rules applicable at once and equally to all. The homeward road cannot be altogether the same for dwellers on the hill and dwellers on the plain ; the goal alone is one.*

The most important and the best known of the special testimonies of which I have now to speak is that which has been steadily borne by our members against all war. Friends have ever maintained and acted upon the belief that war and strife of all kinds are opposed to the spirit and the teaching of Christ, and have felt themselves, as His disciples, precluded from engaging in them.   They have steadfastly refused to take up arms at the bidding of any human authority, or in the presence of any danger.   This course of conduct has, of course, brought them into frequent collision with the civil power, and needs for its justification, as Friends are the first to acknowledge, the warrant of a higher than any national authority.

It is, indeed, an awful position which we have thus been bold to take up—the position of those who feel themselves called upon to act as the salt of the earth, as leaders who refuse to be led.   I do not hesitate to confess that this attitute of possible resistance to the demands of our country in the presence of a common danger was the one part of the Quaker ideal which I for a time seriously hesitated to accept.   So long as I

---

* I hope it will be remembered that my object throughout is to unfold the meaning of our ideal, not at all to estimate the degree in which we actually live according to it.   I am not in a position to form any opinion worth having as to the actual state of the Society, nor if I had any such opinion should I wish to publish it.   My desire is to explain the secret of our strength, not of our weakness.

understood it to be accompanied by or based upon any condemnation of those who conscientiously believe that their duty to God requires them to yield unqualified obedience to the demands of their country for military service I was unable to accept it. But when I came to understand that the Quaker testimony against all war did not take the form of any ethical rule which could be immediately and universally applied, but was simply the acting out in one's own person and at one's own risk of obedience to that which one's own heart had been taught to recognize as Divine authority; even where its commands transcended and came into collision with those of the nation, I felt at once that the position was not only perfectly tenable, but was the only one worthy of faithful disciples.

So long as our country is but very imperfectly Christianized, it is impossible not to recognize that an insuperable contradiction may at any time arise between the demands upon our loyalty and obedience which may be made in its name, and those of the spirit of Christ. It would assuredly not be acting in His spirit to make light of disobedience to law; but neither can any Christian hesitate for a moment when called upon to choose which Master he shall obey. It seems to me that if any man be prepared in the true spirit of a martyr to rise above his country's sense of right, and to serve his country in the highest sense by disobeying and withstanding such of its requirements as in his heart he believes to be wrong and ungodly, it is impossible to withhold from such a man the respect and the admiration which we all feel for the martyrs of old. I do not see how the national standard of duty can be raised—how, in other words the nation can ever be thoroughly Christianized—except through individual faithfulness, at all costs and at all risks to a higher view of duty than that held by the nation at large.

Here of course, we are confronted with the question, *Is* our view of duty truly a higher one than that of the nation at large ? Does the teaching of Jesus Christ really call us to abstain from all warfare ?

It seems to me that not only Friends' testimony, but the teaching of our Master Himself on this subject have been much, and in a sense inevitably, misunderstood. The subject is profoundly complex, and much of what is said and written about it sounds altogether unsubstantial and unpractical, because neither the depth and intricacy of the evil, nor the far-reaching and full significance of the principles opposed to it, are sufficiently felt. " I say unto you, that ye resist not evil : but whosoever shall smite thee on thy right cheek, turn to him the other also." Surely this does not point to an abject submission or a tame indifference, but to an *undaunted* persistence in blessing— a fearless overcoming of evil with good. It is an appeal to an unchanging and fundamental principle, rather than a mere rule of conduct. The whole passage breathes a spirit of ardent confidence in the supremacy of goodness ; in the power of the Perfect One who makes His sun to shine upon the just and the unjust, and sends rain upon the unthankful and the evil ; it is a call to us to be perfect, even as our Father is perfect ;

not a suggestion that we should abandon or relax our conflict with evil, but an assurance that we are not at its mercy—that He who is with us is stronger than all they who can be against us, and that in His strength we can and must meet evil with good and overcome it.

Those who would follow Him who thus spoke, must rise above all personal considerations, and above every temptation to retaliate—not fall below them. This surely was the spirit in which William Penn won his victories in the early days of Pennsylvania—the bloodless victories which make his name to this day a word of love and honour amongst the Indians, with whom his treaty of peace was never broken. It was not by lying down like sheep to be slaughtered by them, but by going forward to meet them with open hands and a trusting heart, and by honourably and generously recognizing their rights, and paying them a fair price for their lands that he and his followers turned suspicion and hatred into firm friendship.

We are called to rise above the level of fighting pagans, not to fall below it. There is, indeed, a lower depth than that of the military spirit—the depth of complacent mammon-worship. To our shame be it confessed that this spirit may clothe itself under the profession of "non-resistance." When the salt so loses its savour, it is truly fit for nothing but to be cast out and trodden under foot. But we are concerned here not with the deplorable caricature of that "testimony against all war" which has for two hundred years been at once the boast and the reproach of Quakerism, but with its essence and true significance. These lie in the fact that Friends have, one by one, individually and unitedly, been led by obedience to the spirit of Christ to abstain from fighting, and from all concern, so far as it has been possible to clear themselves from it, in strife of any kind. This is surely clear and solid ground to take, and quite distinct from any attempt or necessity for laying down general and comprehensive formulæ of conduct applicable to all cases, to all persons and all bodies. To formulate such general rules is, in truth, foreign to the spirit of Quakerism. To yield one's self unreservedly to Divine guidance ; resolutely, and at whatever cost, to refuse to participate in that which one's own conscience has been taught to condemn ;— this is the ancient and inestimable Quaker ideal. It is surely the best, the most effectual, and the most Christian way of witnessing against evil, and of arousing the consciences of others.

There is not, I believe, any possibility of dispute, I will not say amongst Christians, but amongst rational beings, as to the enormity of the evil of strife and discord, whether between nations or between individuals. The question upon which we Friends differ from other Christians is not the question whether peace be desirable —whether it be not, in fact, the goal of all political effort—but what are the means by which it is to be attained or maintained. Other Christians do not deny that quarrelling is contrary to the Spirit of Christ, and we do not deny that a holy warfare is to be continually maintained against evil in every form. But we regard the opposing of violence by violence as a suicidal and hopeless method of proceeding : we feel,

as Christians, that the weapons of our warfare are not
carnal. We cannot, by taking military service, place
ourselves at the absolute disposal of a power which
may at any time employ its soldiers for purposes so
questionable and often so unhallowed.

To abstain, on these grounds, from all participation
in warfare is surely a quite different thing from laying
down any general theory as to the " unlawfulness " of
war. I own that it does not appear to me to be right
or wise to blame those who are acting in obedience to
their own views of duty, however much they may
differ from our own. I do not think it can serve any
good purpose to ignore the force of the considerations
by which war appears to many people to be justified. I
would myself even go further, and admit that, under all
the complicated circumstances of the world (including
historical facts and treaty obligations), there are cases
in which men may be actually bound to fight in what
they believe to be a just cause ; although it does not
I believe, follow that every individual would be justified
in taking part in such warfare. Would any one say
that at the time of the Indian Mutiny the Governor-
General of India ought not to have permitted the use
of arms for the protection of the women and children ?
I doubt whether any Friend would be found to maintain this. But it is equally to be remembered that no
true Friend could well have occupied the position of the
Governor-General. No nation which had from the
beginning of its history been thoroughly Christian
could, I suppose, have found itself in the position which
we occupied in India in 1857. Were all the world, in

the true and full sense of the word, Christian, such events obviously would not occur. Had we been from the first a thoroughly Christian nation, our whole history must have been different, and would (as we Friends believe) have been infinitely nobler.

We do not profess to lay down any general rule, by obedience to which war can be instantly dispensed with by nations in their unregenerate state, and without a sacrifice. A fully Christian nation has never yet been seen on earth. It may well be that such a nation, could it now come suddenly into existence, would meet with national martyrdom. Meanwhile it is the imperfection of our Christianity and the mixed and complex nature of national affairs which make it so difficult to apply to national action any pure principles of conduct. This is not to deny the existence, of such principles. To recognize the difficulty, nay, the impossibility, of suddenly or sweepingly applying them to practice, is not to deny their leavening power. When we Friends speak of what is "right," we refer not to any external and rigid rule of conduct, but to that which in each individual case is truly the best and the highest course open to those concerned. To say this is not to say that right is in itself variable. It is only to say what will, I think, be denied by few, that the human ideal of right is progressive, not stationary.

We do, however, further say, what undoubtedly *is* denied by many, that the ideal revealed to us in the life and the words of Jesus Christ our Lord, and gradually being worked out in His own people through His ever-present inward influence, is the highest and the purest conceivable ; and that, therefore, all real progress must be an approach towards Him. It is this Christian ideal which, as it gains possession of the human mind, must extinguish the spirit which leads to strife and warfare.

It is commonly supposed that Friends have some special scruple about the use of physical force in any case. This is, I believe, by no means true of the Society at large, although the popular notion may very likely be founded upon fact as regards individuals. As a body, Friends have always recognized "the just authority of the civil magistracy," and have, I believe, never disputed the lawfulness of the use of "the sword" (whatever may be meant by that expression) in maintaining that authority.* George Fox himself repeatedly reminded magistrates that they should not "bear the sword in vain," but that they should use it for the punishment of evil-doers, not of those who did well.

It is not, as I understand it, the use of physical force or even the suffering caused by the use of it, which

---

* I believe that scarcely any Friend would be found to consider the office of the policeman as an unlawful one, or to entertain scruples about the use of physical force in maintaining order. I am told that Friends have often, and without censure, acted as special constables.

With regard to the subject of capital punishment, the Yearly Meeting has indeed, during the last 50 years, expressed very serious doubts of its being justifiable ; but the matter is treated as one " needing prayerful consideration " by those whom it may concern, not as beyond all question clear.

really makes war hateful in Christian eyes ; but the evil passions, the "lusts" from which it springs, and to which, alas ! it so hideously ministers. The dispassionate infliction of punishment by an impartial and a lawful authority surely stands upon a quite different footing from that "biting and devouring one another" which, whether between nations or between individuals, it is the very aim and object of law to suppress. Suffering inflicted for the purpose of maintaining peace cannot, I think, be condemned by the advocates of peace unless it be on the ground of failure.

I own that I personally cannot but recognize that upon this view certain wars, or at the least certain acts of warfare, appear to be not only inevitable, but justifiable, as partaking of the nature of national police operations. I cannot, therefore, regard all war as wholly and unmitigatedly blamable, although I can hardly imagine any war which does not both come from evil and lead to evil.

Again, there are treaty obligations requiring us in certain cases to take up arms for the protection of weaker nations, from which we could not suddenly recede without a breach of national good faith. It surely does not become us, in our zeal for peace, to make light of, or overlook such considerations as this. They should, I think, in the first place lead us to abstain from sweeping generalizations, and from blaming those who are ready to lay down their lives in obedience to their country's call and in our defence, or the defence of the oppressed in other countries ; while yet we resolutely maintain our own obedience to that higher authority by which we have, as we believe, been taught a better way—a way incompatible with outward strife—of giving our lives for the common weal. We should be very careful how we call that a wicked action which a good man may honestly do in obedience to his own sense of duty ; we should be still more careful lest, while professing to take higher ground, we do in fact fall far short of such men in our lives ; but we must, for all that, be faithful to the light we have.

And, in the second place, it seems to me that the true inference from the consideration of the complicated conditions of international affairs is that the time is not yet ripe for the assumption of all offices of public authority by thorough-going Christians. Our place surely still is mainly to leaven, not to govern, the world.

The world must become the kingdom of the Lord and of His Christ before wars and fightings will cease from amongst men. And the world is very far as yet from acknowledging that dominion in anything but words. Yet we do " profess and call ourselves Christians " ; we do live in the full light of the ever-lasting gospel ; and however it may be rejected or discarded, however far even those who profess it may be from entering into its spirit, it has yet, in spite of ourselves, raised us out of the possibility of consistent paganism. We cannot return to the old condition of things, in which nations thought it no shame to strive each for its own petty objects, and to be reckless of each other's interests. There is no satisfactory resting-place for us now on any lower level than that which Christ has brought to light.   Under the name of "altruism," this is recognized even by those who think of Christianity as a worn-out superstition.   We who believe it to be the power of God unto salvation are surely bound to yield ourselves heart and soul to its emancipating influence—to its indestructible, irresistible appeal to us to "live as brethren."   As in the beginning it was felt by some at least to be as clear as daylight that " Christians cannot fight," so now, not only amongst Friends, but in many another Christian body, the same spirit is working, and consciences are awakening to the utter incompatibility of strife and retaliation and reckless self-aggrandizement with the spirit of brotherhood which lies at the very foundation of Christianity. They had need to awake ; now, at the eleventh hour, with all Europe making itself ready for war, it may yet be that the few in whom the fire of Christian zeal is burning in its purity may see their cause and the cause of their Master begin to prevail against overwhelming odds.   But whether the nations will hear or whether they will forbear, wherever two or three Christians meet together, there still will be a protest against strife and selfishness.

A protest against strife and selfishness ; not only against strife, but against "the greedy spirit which leads to strife."   If we are willing to go down to the root in this matter, if we truly desire to do what in us lies towards ridding the earth not only of wars and fightings, but of all forms of oppression and cruelty, must we not recognize that the very first step is to bo ourselves freed from covetousness ?

For who can doubt that it is mainly about outward
and material things that nations or individuals are led
into quarrels ?   Who will venture to say that, if none
of us desired either to get or to keep more than our
share of this world's goods, there would be anything
like the amount of fighting, or of preparation for it,
which now devastates the earth ? We may be sceptical
about the possibility of any general acceptance of
arbitration or disarmament.   To be sceptical about the
possibility of personal disinterestedness would imply a
very different sort of blindness.   It seems to me that
in struggling to rise and to raise others more and
more clearly above the greedy spirit which leads to
war, is the best hope for many of us of contributing
in any real sense to the cause of peace on earth.

It was long ago recognized by Friends that (to use
the words of John Woolman) " in every degree of
luxury are the seeds of war and oppression."   The
connection between luxury and cruelty is, indeed,
almost a truism, but it is one of those truisms of which
it is unfortunately easy to lose sight ; and I fear that
even amongst Friends the familiar testimonies against
all war and against superfluities are apt to be held
without any vivid sense of their vital connection.

No one, however, can well deny that the selfish
desire of mere pleasure, when allowed to rule, will feed
itself at the expense of suffering and privation to
others ; that it does cause that scramble for gain in
which the weak are trampled upon, and every furious

passion is stimulated.* The difficulty in regard to bearing a practical testimony against superfluities is not that which some of us feel in the case of war—that we do not know where to take hold, that our personal and daily conduct seems to have no immediate bearing upon questions of international policy, and that the whole problem eludes our grasp by its very vastness. It is, rather, that we do not *like* to put our shoulder to the wheel of simplifying life for ourselves and others; that we do not see the beauty of severity; that we love softness, or yield to it for want of any purifying fire of hope.

But yet, in one form or another, often extravagantly, foolishly, even injuriously, an ineradicable instinct has prompted Christians in all times to free themselves from luxurious and self-indulgent ways of living; to walk as disciples of Him who "had not where to lay His head;" to lay aside, not only every sin, but every weight, that so they may run the race set before them, not as beating the air, but as those who strive for the victory.

It is, indeed, not easy to define the precise kind or amount of indulgence which is incompatible with Christian simplicity; or rather it must of necessity vary. But the principle is, I think, clear. In life, as

---

° It is, I believe, notorious that many of the panics which often actually lead to war, and which tend to keep up the enormous and demoralizing burdens of an "armed peace," are largely brought about by those who have a pecuniary interest in them, either for stock-jobbing or for newspaper-selling interests.

in art, whatever does not help, hinders. All that is superfluous to the main object of life must be cleared away, if that object is to be fully attained. In all kinds of effort, whether moral, intellectual or physical, the essential condition of vigour is a severe pruning away of redundance. Is it likely that the highest life, the life of the Christian body, can be carried on upon easier terms?

The higher our ideal of life, the greater, indeed, must be the sacrifices which it will require from us. As we rise from the lower to the higher objects of life, many things of necessity become superfluous to us—in other words, we become independent of them, or outgrow them. This is a widely different idea from that of ascetic self-discipline or self-mortification ; and it is surely a sounder and a worthier idea.

The Quaker ideal, as I understand it, requires a continual weighing of one thing against another—a continual preference of the lasting and deep over the transient and superficial. "Weightiness" is one of the Friends' characteristic and emphatic forms of commendation. To sacrifice any deep and substantial advantage to outward show is abhorrent to the Quaker instinct. To "stretch beyond one's compass," grasping at shadows, and encumbering oneself with more than is needed for simple, wholesome living, is at variance with all our best traditions.

If we bear in mind the essentially relative meaning of the word "superfluous," it is obvious that such a testimony against "superfluities" does not require any rigid or niggardly rule as to the outward things. To my own mind, indeed, this view of the matter seems to require at least as clearly the liberal use of whatever is truly helpful to "our best life" as the abandonment of obstructing superfluities. No doubt a testimony against superfluities is very liable to degenerate into formality, and to be so misapplied as to cut off much that is in reality wholesome, innocent, and beautiful. Art has to a great extent been banished from many Quaker homes ; and a considerable amount of injury has no doubt been done by such rigid severity, and perhaps still more by the very natural consequent reaction. But it would, I believe, be quite a mistake to suppose that the extreme plainness in dress and other surroundings adopted by the stricter Friends, and formerly made a matter of discipline by the Society, was originally adopted with any intention of self-mortification and asceticism.*

I believe that asceticism is in a very deep sense contrary to the real Quaker spirit, which desires in all things to abstain from any interference "in the will of man" with Divine discipline and guidance, and which would, I believe, regard the idea of self-chosen exercises in mortification of the flesh with the same aversion as it entertains for pre-arranged forms of worship. Friends, no doubt, have often believed themselves required to submit to the adoption of the plain

---

* I mean by "asceticism" the practice of any humanly devised religious or spiritual discipline, whether self-chosen or prescribed by authority.

I

dress " in the cross " to natural inclination, and have felt it a valuable exercise to do so ; but the plainness was not devised for that purpose, but chosen (or rather, as Friends would say, they were led into it by Truth) because of its inherent suitableness and rightness.   It is an outcome of the instinctively felt necessity of subordinating everything to principle. Its chief significance is that of a protest against bondage to passing fashions, and for this reason it is a settled costume.   It is also felt that our very dress should show forth that inward quietness of spirit which does not naturally tend towards outward adornment, and the Friends' recognized dress is therefore out of extreme sobriety in colour and simplicity in form.

It is a significant fact that there is really no such thing as a precisely defined Quaker costume.   The dress certainly looks precise enough in itself, and to the naked eye of the outside observer it may appear to present an undeviating uniformity : but it is really not a uniform in the sense in which a nun's or a soldier's dress is a uniform.   It is in all respects a growth, a tradition, a language : and it is subject to constant though slow modification. Any perfectly unadorned dress of quiet colour, without ornament or trimming, if habitually worn, is in fact, to all intents and purposes, the Quaker costume, though one or two details have by a sort of accident acquired a traditional meaning as a Ladge, which one may adopt or not according to one's feeling about badges.   Some Friends now-a-days object on principle to anything of the kind.   Others still see a " hedge " or shelter in them.   Others, again, feel that they serve a useful and innocent purpose in enabling Friends readily to recognize one another, and that it is not amiss for them to be easily recognized even by outsiders. But the one important matter of principle which the Society as a body have recognized, is that it is a waste of time and money for which Christian women can hardly fail to find better employment, to condescend to be perpetually changing the fashion of one's garments in obedience to the caprice or the restlessness of the multitude. "Plain Friends" are those who are resolved to dress according to the settled principles which commend themselves to their own minds, not enslaving themselves to passing fashions.

It is easy to say that they do but exchange one bondage for another. That may, indeed, have been the case at times, and may even still be so in some families or meetings. But the crystallizing into rigid formality, though a possible tendency, is no real part of the true Quaker ideal. My own strong feeling is that the adoption of a settled costume, at any rate in mature life and from conviction, is not only the right and most dignified course on moral grounds, but also that it has in actual experience afforded one more proof of the truth that the lower aims of life can thrive only in proportion as they are kept in subordination to the higher. The freedom from the necessity of perpetual changes, which commends itself to Friends as suitable to the dignity of "women professing godliness," has also the lower advantage of admitting a gradual bringing to perfection of the settled costume itself. We all know how exquisite, within its severely limited range, can be the result. The spotless delicacy, the precision and perfection of plain fine needlework, the repose of the soft tints, combine, in the dress of some still lingering representatives of the old school of Quakerism, to produce a result whose quiet beauty appeals to both the mind and the eye with a peculiar charm. I cannot think that such mute eloquence is to be despised; or that it is unworthy of Christian women to be careful that their very dress shall speak a language of quietness, gentleness, and purity—that it shall be impressed even with a touch of eternity.

This principle of Christian simplicity should, in our view, run through everything—dress, furniture, habits of life, and forms of speech; all should be severely purged from redundance, and from mere imitation and conventionality. The "plain language," best known as leading to the use of *thee* and *thou* for *you* in speaking to one person, and of first, second, etc., for the days of the week and the months, instead of the ordinary names "derived from heathen deities," was an instance of this endeavour to winnow away every superfluity and every taint of flattery and superstition from our speech. These special peculiarities of speech are, as is well known, completely dropped by many of the present generation of Friends. The changes which have taken place in two hundred years in our language and habits have deprived these expressions of much of their original significance, and the tendency of the present time is no doubt towards the effacing of all peculiarities. But some special attention is still paid amongst us to simplicity and guardedness of language in a wider sense, and surely this is an object well worthy of attention on the highest as well as the lowest grounds.

The idea of a scrupulous guard over the lips, which is so strongly characteristic of all Friends at all worthy of the name, culminates in their united testimony against oaths. This has, indeed, been always regarded by Friends as a matter of simple obedience to a plain command of Jesus Christ ; and I think that nothing but long habit could reconcile any sincere disciple to the ordinary interpretation of His words as intended to forbid "profane swearing" only.* Many others besides Friends have felt this scruple ; but to our Society belongs the indisputable credit of having, through a long and severe course of suffering for their "testimony," obtained a distinct recognition of the sufficiency in their case of a plain affirmation, thereby vindicating a principle which is beginning to be generally recognized—the principle of having but one rule for all cases, that of plain truth ; of being as much bound by one's word as one's bond. I think it can hardly be questioned that, through this simple and unflinching course of obedience to the plain injunction of Jesus Christ, Friends have done much to raise the standard of veracity in our country.†

---

* "But I say unto you, Swear not at all. . . . But let your communication be, Yea, yea ; Nay, nay : for whatsoever is more than these cometh of evil" (Matt. v. 34-37).

† The victory thus won by Friends has paved the way for greater liberty for all ; and at the present time any one (whether

The refusal to pay tithes is a part of the testimony against a paid ministry, of which I have sufficiently spoken in the last chapter ; and I need here only say that in all these cases of resistance to the demands of authority, for military service, for oaths, or for tithes, the idea has been that of witnessing at one's own cost against unjust or unrighteous demands. It is, I think, fair to claim that it is at one's own cost that one refuses a demand even for money when it is made by those who have the power to take the money or its equivalent by force, and when no resistance is ever offered to their doing so.   Friends have again and again submitted patiently to the levying of much larger sums than those originally claimed, as well as to severe and sometimes lifelong imprisonments, and other penalties, rather than by any act of their own give consent to exactions which they believed to be unrighteous in their origin or purpose.   While such unmistakable proofs of disinterestedness were given, the motive for witholding money could hardly be misunderstood. With regard to tithes, however, the circumstances have, since the Tithes Commutation Act, become so complicated, that few Friends now feel a refusal to pay them a suitable method of testifying against a paid ministry, and the Yearly Meeting has placed on record this sense of the alteration of the state of the case in a minute dated 1875 : * "This meeting believes that the time has

___

"professing with us" or not) who objects on the ground of religion to the taking of an oath is equally at liberty to affirm.

° "Book of Discipline," p. 141.

arrived when the mode of bearing this testimony must be left to the individual consciences of Friends."

Amongst lesser matters as to which Friends have made a stand upon principle against prevailing customs may be mentioned "the superstitious observance of days," especially that of fasts or thanksgivings prescribed by the civil government (a power which we do not regard as competent to prescribe religious exercises), and the practice of wearing mourning, and placing "inscriptions of a eulogistic character" on tomb-stones. In Friends' burial-grounds nothing beyond the name, and the dates of birth and death, is permitted. The objections to wearing mourning are obvious, both on the ground of unnecessary expense and trouble at a time when the mind should surely be left as much as possible undisturbed, and also on that of its being an expression (and an expression so formal as to be of doubtful sincerity) of grief and gloom in regard to providential dispensations which, however painful, we should desire to accept with cheerful submission. There is obviously much to be said for this application of the principle of simplifying our customs, and adjusting our dress and other surroundings to the permanent rather than the transient circumstances of our lives.

To simplify life to the very uttermost—is not this truly in itself a worthy aim ; nay, the one inexorable condition of excellence ?

We have just now been engaged with comparatively trivial matters—straws which show as no more solid thing can do which way the wind blows. These things are important, not in themselves, but in relation to the principles in honest obedience to which they have been worked out. Simplicity—"the simplicity which is in Christ "—the simplicity, not of exclusion, but of Divine, all-subduing supremacy—this is the key-note of our ideal ; and it is a key-note to which the human heart must always in some degree respond. At the bottom of all art, of all beauty, and surely, we may say, of all goodness, lies the principle of subordination—the necessity of a perpetual choice between the permanent and the transient, the essential and the superficial. Quakerism is an honest endeavour to carry out this principle in the Christian life ; to weigh "in the balance of the sanctuary" the meat that endureth against the meat that perisheth ; to cleave to the eternal at the sacrifice, if necessary, of all that is temporal.

I am, of course, not absurd enough to claim that this endeavour is peculiar to Quakerism. My object throughout is to show what are the eternal and unassailable principles of truth to which Quakerism appeals, to which it clings as to its strongholds. And I believe that the severe sifting away of non-essentials which lies at the foundation of our revolt from accepted ecclesiastical practices, and which has ramified in detail into these minor testimonies, often rigidly and at times even laughably worked out by individuals, is a process more and more urgently needed in these days of rapid growth in all material and intellectual resources.

The permanent danger of giving our labour and our lives "for that which satisfieth not " was surely never more desperate than in these days of hurry and fulness, when merely to stand still needs a resolute effort of will. Are not half the lives we know carried along in a current they know not how to resist towards objects they but vaguely recognize, and in their heart of hearts do not value? Was the bondage of outward things even more oppressive than it is to many of those who are ostensibly, and ought to be really, in a position of entire outward independence? How many of us have attained to the unspeakable repose of having our centre of gravity in the right place, of leaning upon nothing that can fail?

There is no royal road to ridding ourselves of super-fluities. It is a lifelong process of severe purification, which at every turn demands the sacrifice of the lower to the higher. But as this severity is the necessary price of attaining what is highest, so also it is the one spell by which life and significance and value can be given to what is lower. If it burns it also brightens; while it destroys it irradiates. I believe it to be in all things true that nothing can have its full value except when rightly subordinated to that which is of more importance than itself. If you sacrifice the higher to the lower, you not only make a bad bargain, but you injure the very object which you thus purchase. That of which you make an idol turns to dust in the process. The idol which you have the courage to pluck from its throne may come to life through that very act. From the closest human affection down to the most trivial outward adornment, all lovely things owe their perfection of loveliness to being held in their due subordination to what is yet higher. " He that will lose his life shall save it ; " a hard saying, indeed—with the hardness of the imperishable rock in which is our fortress and our stronghold.

CHAPTER VI.

OUR CALLING.

I HAVE endeavoured to explain what are those principles and practices into which we as a body have been led through what we believe to be obedience to the Spirit of Truth. I know that in some respects we seem to our fellow Christians to have mistaken the voice of our Guide, and to be, through ignorance perhaps, but yet lamentably, excluding ourselves from the most precious privileges, if not consciously disregarding the most sacred injunctions. It is a very solemn question upon which we thus join issue with almost all the Churches of Christendom ;—What is, in fact, essential Christianity ?

" By their fruits ye shall know them." It would ill become me to attempt any estimate of the fruitfulness of that branch of the Christian Church which I have joined as compared with the branch of it in which I was brought up. I have been occupied throughout with our ideal, not with the degree of our fulfilment or failure to fulfil it. I feel bound, however, to say that I cannot reconcile the fact of the signs of life and spiritual energy which I find within as well as without the Society with the idea that either branch of the

Church is really cut off from the root of the living Vine. Does it follow that our peculiar principles and practices are of no consequence ?

I cannot myself believe that this is a legitimate conclusion from the admitted fact that undeniably holy and Christian lives are led within as well as without our borders. That fact does, I think, show at least that everything does not depend either upon the observance or the disuse of outward ordinances—it shows that either course may be pursued in good faith and without destruction to the Christian life ; but it is not inconsistent with the belief that results of profound importance to the character of our Christianity are involved in this question of ordinances and orders, and that it therefore behoves us to seek the utmost clearness with regard to it.

This question is the very key of the position of the Society of Friends as a separate body. It it as witnesses to the independence of spiritual life upon outward ordinances that we believe ourselves especially called to maintain our place in the universal Church in the present day.

The importance of our separate position is perhaps somewhat obscured in the eyes of some amongst us by the fact that we can no longer assume the vehemently aggressive attitude of the early Friends, as against Christians of other denomiations. They believed it to be their duty to attack the "hireling priests" of their day as guilty of "apostasy," and upholders of the mysterious powers of darkness. In our own day such judgments would imply either the grossest ignorance

or else downright insanity. We cannot help knowing,
and rejoicing to know, that a large proportion of the
clergy are amongst the most devoted and disinterested
of the children of light, using their official position, as
well as every other power of body and mind, for the
promotion of the kingdom of God and the spread of
the gospel. We desire nothing better than to fight
beside them, shoulder to shoulder, against the common
enemy : and we are in fact often associated with them
in efforts of this kind.

In like manner, it would be impossible for Friends
in these days to speak in the tone of the founders of the
Society, as though we possessed a degree of light in
comparison of which all other Christians must be
considered as groping in thick darkness. The early
Friends sometimes spoke of the " breaking forth of the
gospel day " through the revelation made to them as
of an event almost equal in importance to its original
promulgation sixteen hundred years before. In these
days we could not with any kind of honesty or justice
claim a position so enormously in advance of our
neighbours. On all hands we see evidences of fidelity
and fruitfulness, and the shining of examples which
we rejoice to admire, and desire to emulate.

There is thus, I think, a certain perplexity as to our
relative position in the Christian Church which is a
cause of some weakness amongst Friends. It is in
some respects easier to maintain an aggressive attitude
than one of mere quiet separateness ; and it would
be no wonder if some, especially of our younger
members, in these days of free interchange of sympathy,

should begin to falter a little as to the importance of our separate position. It is, indeed, one which will not be maintained except as the result of deep and searching spiritual discipline. The testimony against dependence on what is outward cannot be borne to any purpose at second hand. We must ourselves be weaned from all hankering after what is outward and tangible before we can appreciate the value of a testimony to the sufficiency of the purely spiritual; and that weaning is not an easy process, nor one that can be transmitted from generation to generation. Unless our younger Friends be taught in the same stern school as their forefathers, they will assuredly not maintain the vantage-ground won by the faithfulness of a former generation.

Some other causes have, I believe, tended to confuse our relation to the outer world, and make it important that Friends should look well to their path, and consider whither it is tending: whether we are really guarding the position which it is specially our business to defend, or allowing ourselves to be drawn off into the pursuit of less important matters. There are in the main stream of the Society many currents and counter currents, and its recent history has been one of change and reaction, so that it would be dangerous and presumptuous for a new-comer to attempt to foretell its course; but I may venture to point out some of the tendencies which are and have been at work amongst us, preparing the conditions under which our future work must be done.

It is well known that the Society, which sprang very

rapidly into existence in the middle of the seventeenth century, began during the eighteenth to diminish in numbers, and was for many years a steadily dwindling body. Closed meeting-houses and empty benches are now to be found in all parts of the country where, in former days, the difficulty was to find room for all who came. Within the last thirty or forty years our numbers have, however, begun slowly to increase, although the increase is so far from being equal to the rate of increase of the population at large, that in proportion to other denominations we may still be considered as in a certain sense losing ground. The actual increase, small as it is, is nevertheless a significant fact.*

The great falling-off in numbers during the eighteenth and part of the nineteenth centuries was probably caused, in part at least, by the fact that after the early days of growth and persecution there followed a time of outward quietness, in which the value attached to what one may call Quaker tradition became excessive, and resulted in too rigid a discipline. The actual discipline of the Society was applied with a strictness which surely was not altogether wise or wholesome ; and the less tangible restraint of public opinion within the borders of a small and very exclusive sect was probably even more oppressive in its rigidity and minuteness of supervision. Until within the last thirty years or thereabouts, it was the almost invariable practice to

---

* The number of members was reported in 1862 as 13,844 ; in 1889 as 15,574. Before 1862 no returns were made.

disown all members who married " out of Society," and this restriction must obviously have done much not only to diminish the numbers, but probably also to alienate the affections of successive rising generations. So many of the young people lost or resigned their membership for this and other causes, that, had no change taken place, the days of the Society must to all appearance have been numbered.

But in the early part of this century, owing, in a great measure to the influence of Joseph John Gurney and his sister, Elizabeth Fry, a new wave of religious and benevolent activity arose ; and about the same time, though with what degree of connection with this impulse I do not know, a considerable relaxation of discipline took place.   Not only was the practice with regard to marriages out of the Society relaxed, but many minor matters, in which an irksome and, no doubt, often hurtful rigidity had prevailed, began to be deliberately left to the judgment of individuals.   In 1861 a revision of the " Book of Discipline " took place, which reflected and sanctioned the relaxation of super-vision in regard to these matters.   In that year the latter part of the fourth query, relating to "plainness of speech, behaviour, and apparel," was dropped, and other changes were made in the queries then in use.   The Yearly Meeting, as has been already mentioned, no longer requires that any of the queries should be answered, except those which regard the regularity with which meetings are held and attended.   These changes have meant in practice that the maintenance of all our special " testimonies " is now (like that against tithes)

" left to the individual conscience," and not inquired
into by the meetings for discipline ; and the immediate
result has, of course, been a great outward and visible
alteration—a rapid disappearance of distinguishing
peculiarities, and no doubt an immense relief to the
younger members.

A more direct result of the " evangelical " influence of
the Gurneys, and others like-minded, was the setting-in
of a current of activity in all sorts of benevolent, philanthropic, and missionary directions. The old dread of
" creaturely activity,"—of moving in any kind of
religious work without an immediate prompting and
even constraining influence from above,—seems to have
in some degree given place to a fear of burying our
talent. The Christian duty of going forth to seek and
to save, of holding forth the word of life, and letting
our light shine before men, had been beautifully exem-
plified by some eminent men and women in the Society.
Many of the younger Friends caught the flame of their
zeal, and from all quarters, in these modern days, influences combine to make that " sitting still," in which
an earlier generation of Friends had found their
strength, appear almost an impossibility.

With the new rising tide of fervent zeal and benevo-
lence came a great change in the prevailing tone of
religious feeling. The Bible, which, in their dread
lest the letter should usurp the place of the spirit, had
amongst Friends been almost put under a bushel, was
brought into new prominence, and so-called " evangelical " views respecting the unique or exceptional
nature of its inspiration began to be entertained.

Gradually the idea of the necessity of teaching " sound doctrine " assumed an importance which had formerly been reserved for that of looking for " right guidance ; " and in some quarters a visible tendency has, of late years, been manifest towards more definition of doctrines and popularizing of methods than would have been tolerated half a century ago.*

Although these modern tendencies have undoubtedly been accompanied by, and have probably in some degree led to, an increase in our numbers, a strong protest has from time to time been raised against them by those who feel that Quakerism had its roots and its strength in a deep inward and spiritual experience which frees from all dependence upon outward things. In America the protest against (or, as those who protest would no doubt rather say, the introduction of) this modern phase of comparatively superficial religious activity has caused grievous schisms and troubles. About the year 1826, a large party, under the leadership of one Elias Hicks, in that country broke off altogether from the main body of Friends, and is suspected by the " orthodox " of having, under professed obedience to the inner light, become practically a Unitarian or rationalist body. In England, however, the two main

---

* Many other causes have, no doubt, been at work in bringing about the changes referred to in the text. I am, indeed, not qualified to attempt anything like an adequate account, on however slight a scale, of the recent history of the Society, and have desired in this passage only to indicate the general direction of the principal division of parties amongst us.

currents have flowed side by side, and have not resulted in any considerable division of the stream.

Both parties claim to be taking their stand upon the original principles of the early Friends. Those who uphold above all things the doctrine of the inward light, and the primary necessity of immediate inspiration and guidance to the bringing forth of any good word or work, and especially to the performance of any acceptable worship, have abundant evidence to produce, in the writings of Fox, Barclay, Penn, Penington, and other fathers of the Society, that this was the foundation and the constant burden of all their teaching. Those, on the other hand, who are throwing themselves heart and soul into missionary and "evangelistic" efforts, say truly enough that the early Friends did not so "wait for guidance" as to be content to sit still and make no effort to lighten the darkness around them, and that it was the intermediate or "mediæval," not the "primitive" teaching of the Society which exalted the individual consciousness into the supreme authority, thus developing, in fact, a claim to something approaching personal infallibility.

There are, of course, dangers in either extreme—in the over-valuation of visible and tangible activity, and in the undue intensity of introspective quietism. Too much "inwardness" seems to develop an extraordinary bitterness and spirit of judgment, under the shadow of which no fresh growth would be possible. It is obviously dangerous to sanity. Too much "outwardness" dilutes and destroys the very essence of our testimony, encourages a worthless growth of human

dependence, and can hardly fail to be dangerous to
sincerity. But yet the divergence is, I believe, a case
rather of diversity of gifts and functions than of
contradiction in principle. Both functions are surely
needed. Where a living fountain is really springing
up within, it must needs tend to overflow. The leaves
and blossoms are as essential to the health and fruitfulness of a tree as its root. The secret, as I believe, of
the strength of our Society, its peculiar qualification
for service in these days, lies in its strong grasp of the
oneness of the inward and the outward, as well as in
the deep and pure spirituality of its aim in regard to
both.

There is, I believe and am sure, a special and urgent
need in these days for that witness to the light—light
both within and without—which was the special office
of early Quakerism. I am not equally sure that
Quakerism, as it is, is the vehicle best adapted to convey
that testimony to the present generation. If it be not
so, it is largely the fault of our degeneracy as a body ;
of the lapse of our Society into a rigid formalism
during the eighteenth century, and into a shallow
seeking for popularity in the nineteenth. But, in spite
of all such right-hand and left-hand defections, it
seems to me that there is life enough yet in the old tree
for a fresh growth of fruit-bearing branches. It seems
to me that the framework of the Society has vigour and
elasticity enough yet to be used as an invaluable instrument by a new generation of fully convinced Friends,
were our younger members but fully willing and
resolved to submit to the necessary Divine discipline.

It is no new wave of "creaturely activity," no judicious adapting of Quakerism to modern tastes, that will revive its power in the midst of the present generation. It is a fresh breaking forth of the old power, the unchanging and unchangeable power of light and truth itself, met and invited by a fresh submission of heart in each one of us, which can alone invigorate what is languishing amongst us, and make us more than ever a blessing to the nation.

Had this power ever wholly disappeared from amongst us, there would be little use in dwelling fondly upon its deserted tenement. It is because a measure of the ancient spirit is still to be recognized amongst our now widely scattered remnant that I would fain stir it up, amongst our own members especially, and if possible also amongst others, by means of the experience actually acquired by our Society of the power of an exclusively spiritual religion.

It is, I hope, hardly necessary to repeat that it is not Quakerism, but Truth, that I desire to serve and to promote ; the sect may no longer be what is needed, and may be destined to extinction, for ought I know. But that view of Truth which has found in Quakerism its most emphatic assertion,—that purely spiritual worship and that supremacy of the light within which were set forth with power by Fox and Barclay and Penington,—these things are of perennial value and efficacy, and the need for their fresh recognition seems to be in our own day peculiarly urgent.

There can, indeed, be no rivalry between inward and outward light. Light, we know, is one, and there

can be no contradiction between its various manifesta-
tions, although there may, of course, be any amount of
contradiction between the respective visions of different
people. It seems, indeed, as idle to look for an absolutely colourless medium within as without, in our
own hearts as in the Bible or the Church ; and upon
each one lies the responsibility of accepting correction
from all quarters. Yet for each one of us there must
be a final authority ; and I do not see how that authority
can be found elsewhere than in the Presence dwelling
in the inmost chamber of our own hearts, for it is by
that authority alone that we can be justified even in
choosing any external guide. It is, indeed, impossible
for any one who recognizes the shining of light within
to doubt its supreme authority.

To speak of light shining in one's own heart as something not conclusive for oneself would be almost a contradiction in terms. But just because it *is* within one's
own heart, its range is strictly limited. My inner light
can be no rule (though in a sense it may be as a lamp)
for any one else, for the very reason which forbids me
to dispute it. Each one surely owes an exclusive
allegiance to that ray of Divine light which shines
straight into his own inmost sanctuary.

It is, therefore, no disloyalty to the light within to
acknowledge the need of an outward standard for purposes of united action or mutual judgment, or to accept
an outward test of the reality of our possession of inward
light. Those who have learnt to recognize in the light
within the radiance of the Divine Word will acknowledge no lower voice as the supreme authority without ;

and will accept no other test of its reality than that assigned by Christ himself—righteousness of life.

Friends have always without hesitation accepted the Bible as the one common standard by which their practice and their teaching should be tried,* and have acknowledged from the first that no claim to Divine inspiration could be justified except by the actual possession of the righteousness taught by Christ Himself in word and in deed—a righteousness "exceeding that of the scribes and Pharisees."

And here we come upon the fact, not always sufficiently remembered, that the indispensable words "inward" and "outward" need care in the handling.

° Robert Barclay, who was for generation after generation regarded as the main pillar of theoretic Quakerism, plainly declares the Scriptures to be "a secondary rule"—subordinate, that is, to the teaching of the Spirit by which they were given forth. He anticipates many now familiar reflections about the inherent uncertainties of interpretation and application which preclude the possibility of our finding in any written words a sufficient guide in the infinite variety of individual circumstances ; and also recognizes fully the many sources of error appertaining to writings so ancient, and derived through so many differing versions and translations. He declares, however, that "because they are commonly acknowledged by all to have been written by the dictates of the Holy Spirit, and that the errors which may be supposed by the injury of Times to have slipt in are not such but that there is a sufficient clear Testimony left to all the essentials of the Christian faith, we do look upon them as the only fit outward judge of controversies amongst Christians," and adds that "we are very willing that all our doctrines and practices shall be tried

It is of great importance to my whole subject that the different senses in which they may be applied should be kept in mind.   I have already* pointed out that the mystical meaning of "within" or "inwardness" is not the only one upon which we insist.

This well-known Quaker watchword must always be understood as asserting not only that light is to be found by retiring into the inmost chamber of one's own heart, but also that it is intrinsic, essential, original ; that being inwardly revealed, it must, if real, illuminate the whole being. Righteousness, the fruit and result of obedience to light, is in this sense both inward and outward : it is external, but not extraneous ; outward in the sense of being visible, tangible, open to the light of day—a thing which, however it may be defined or accounted for, is universally recognizable, and is acknowledged by all as justifying the teaching which produces it ; it is not outward in the sense of coming from without, or of being in any degree arbitrary, or accidental, or

---

by them ;" and that " we shall also be very willing to admit, as a positive certain maxim, *That whatsoever any do, pretending to the Spirit, which is contrary to the Scriptures, be accounted and reckoned a Delusion of the Devil.* For as we never lay claim to the Spirit's leadings that we may cover ourselves in anything that is evil ; so we know, that as every evil contradicts the Scriptures, so it doth also the Spirit in the first place, from which the Scriptures came" (Barclay's "Apology," p. 86 : London, 1736).

° "The Inner Light," pp. 23-26.

dependent upon the judgment of our fellow creatures ; it is a natural, not an artificial, test and result of the inward state.   Neither is it outward in the sense of appertaining only to what is visible.   It does, indeed, impress its stamp even upon the very frame, and of course it consists largely in a visible and real dominion of the mind over the body ; but it is, in its origin and essence, of the spirit, not of the flesh.

It was the constant and vigorous seeking for and application of this test of righteousness which distinguished the early Friends from mere mystics. Those " Friends of the Light " were not content to brood over a light shut in to their own hearts.   They let it shine freely before men, boldly proclaiming its universality, and calling all men to walk in it.   They stoutly claimed that it was the light of Jesus Christ of Nazareth, the very Sun of Righteousness, and that the light, spirit, and grace of Christ in their own hearts was one with the spirit in which the Scriptures were given forth. Above all, they insisted that the light was the Spirit of Truth, and must lead into all truth ; not into omniscience or infallibility, but into truth in the inmost parts—truth in word, in thought, and in deed.   Thus they recognized the great truth that the light within and the light without are alike aspects of the Eternal Word of God—that Word which, abiding in us, is our Eternal Life.

Light within—not the vision of the mystic alone, but cleanness of heart, uprightness, sincerity, singleness of mind—of this light they affirmed that every living soul has some germ, which, as it was attended to, would lead out of the evil it condemned. And the glory of their teaching was that it summoned each human spirit to work out its own salvation—in fear and in trembling truly, and in the strength of God working with and in it, but without dependence on any human being, or on anything perishable, or disputable, or accidental ; to repent, and to bring forth fruits meet for repentance ; to walk soberly, as children of the day.

This is what I mean by the pure spirituality of the *aim* of Friends both as to the inward and the outward. The inner light they desire to walk in is not an intellectual but a purifying light : it consists not in rapture, ecstasy, sensation, but in clear insight into the deepest kind of truth : it leads not to knowledge, but to holiness,—which is, indeed, knowledge of the truth. It shines in quietness : and in order to cherish it we must lay aside our preoccupation with the vivid and clamorous and transitory things that are without, dwelling in stillness upon what is eternal, that all things may be revealed in their true proportions. It courts and acknowledges an outward test : but that test consists in the quality of its own outward results as commending themselves to every man's conscience, and reveals itself not in a conformity to other people's teaching, but in a transforming power. The outward stamp we value is not a stamp or sign applied or administered from without and by material means, but the outward and visible radiance of the flame kindled within. The supremacy of the light within as recognized by us in the supremacy of the fountain over the stream, and the cleanness and cleansing power of the stream is the proof of the purity of the fountain. It is in fixing attention upon moral and spiritual results, rather than upon precision of doctrine or correctness of ceremonial observance, that Friends have, I believe, hit the right nail on the head. In our own day, as in George Fox's day, this direct appeal to conscience is surely the one unfailing means by which men and women can be "turned to the light," brought to recognize Him who is the Light, and taught to find in Him their everlasting rest—the rest which is the beginning of power and of victory.

If we be right in our belief that the salvation of Jesus Christ is a purely spiritual influence, a flame which finds in every human heart some prepared fuel, and which is to be spread from heart to heart as fire is kindled from torch to torch ; which is to be maintained not by rites and ceremonies, and "the apostolical succession" of outward ordination, but by that turning from dead works to serve the living God which is in the power of every living soul, and which no one can perform for another ;—if this view be true, then Friends have yet a great work to do in promulgating it, and a great responsibility in having received it as an inheritance.

For this is not yet the commonly accepted view. The Christianity which has spread and flourished is still deeply saturated with reliance upon outward rites and outward ordinances, and deeply entangled with rigid formularies. It is largely composed of creeds and doctrines, which, whether theoretically true or false, are yet capable of being held in unrighteousness, and incapable, therefore, of truly redeeming the souls who trust in them.

Most Christians say or assume that these things are vitally helpful to them. I dare not presume to say that they are wrong, though I own that I think the assumption too conventional to be conclusive. But of one thing I am quite sure. There is a great and increasing multitude amongst us who cannot accept outward rites or clerical teaching. We see by the experience of Roman Catholic countries how inevitable the spread of priestly influence amongst devout women is accompanied by the utter alienation of thinking men from religion itself. I fear that a tendency of the same kind is visible in England now. What is the proportion of men to women to be seen in the congregations of London Churches ? Is it not obvious even to our outward senses that there is something in modern Christianity which the masculine mind rejects ? We have, indeed, abundant proof in the literature of our day that this is the case. Are we driven to conclude that it is the essence of the religion of Jesus Christ which is rejected by masculine thought ; or does the stumbling-block lie in human additions to the teaching of Christ Himself ?

I cannot doubt, and I believe few of the worthiest representatives of masculine thought would deny, that His own teaching, as we have it in the Gospels, is eternal truth : as secure against every storm of doubt and revolt as the sun in heaven is secure against the whirlwind. The Christianity of Jesus Christ Himself is the Christianity upon which Friends alone, or almost

alone, have boldly taken their stand as all-sufficient.
In preaching this essential Christianity we can appeal
with boldness to the witness in every human heart :
and I venture to say that it is not a religion for women
and children only, but one which appeals to and
fortifies the best instincts of manly independence.*

Let it not be supposed that I attribute the whole of
the modern revolt from religion to the engrafting of
ecclesiastical "developments" upon the simplicity
which is in Christ.   I know, of course, that many other
forces tend to alienate men (and women too) from God,
and that there is much in the progress of scientific
discovery which it is difficult to reconcile quickly with
even the very essence of religion.   It is because the

---

* It may be worth while to mention in this connection that
there is not, so far as I have observed, any habitual preponderance
of women in Friends' meetings.   This impression is confirmed by
the fact that the number of habitual "attenders" (non-members)
at our meetings is given (in the tabular statement prepared for
the Yearly Meeting of 1880) as follows :—

Males..............................	2,962
Females............................	3,086
	6,048

For a list of these meetings for worship now held in London, see
Appendix, Note D.

The rapid growth of Friends' First Day Adult Schools is another
significant fact, as showing the openness to the teaching and
influence of Friends amongst working men, and at the same time
the energetic way in which that influence is being used.   This
movement began, at the suggestion of the late Joseph Sturge, in

ship of faith is in danger that I long to see it lightened of unnecessary burdens. It is because men are ready enough to cast from them all thought of the things which belong to their peace, and to abandon in despair the hope which alone can purify their lives, that I long to see that hope disentangled from whatever is worn out and cumbersome and unreasonable.

Quakerism in its origin was a bold and successful struggle to do this. The glory of early Quakerism was in its integrity, in its uncompromising, unflinching requirement that the life should bear witness to the truth, and its resolute stand against any other requirement. The "light within" was not only a word of the deepest poetical and mystical significance : it was a doctrine of sternest righteousness, and at the same time an assertion of resolute independence. Those who were conscious of the shining of Divine light into their own hearts needed no priestly absolution or

---

Birmingham in 1845 ; and it appears from the annual report of the Friends' First Day School Association, that the number of adult scholars was in March, 1889, as follows :—

Men	17,591
Women	5,535
	23,126

The Society of Friends, it should be remembered, numbers (including children) only 15,574 members, yet the teaching in these schools is entirely undertaken by Friends personally, and is, I believe, done altogether without paid help, though valuable assistance is in many cases given by former scholars.

interposition. They were willing to stand or fall by their innocence in the sight of all men. Their very gaolers often trusted them to convey themselves to their distant prisons if they had but promised. It was well known in those early days that a Friend's word was as good as his bond; and to this very day a reputation for special truthfulness and sobriety clings to them, and not, I believe, without reason.

I am anxious to insist upon the resolution to maintain a high moral standard amongst us, not only because of the supreme intrinsic importance of righteousness; not only because I believe that as religion is cleared of outward and ceremonial and perishable elements this indestructible growth of holiness has more room to expand; but also because it cannot be denied, and should, indeed, never be forgotten, that there is very real ground for the suspicion, or, at any rate, the jealous scrutiny, with which any peculiarly exalted spiritual aspirations are apt to be regarded.

There is a well-known and very awful connection between religious emotion and emotions arising from sources less pure. There is an ever-present danger lest in any endeavour to stimulate the one we should rouse the other, and a still worse danger lest the lower should assume the garb and appearance of the higher. The history of religious revivals affords abundant warning of the dangers inseparable from all sudden outbursts of feeling, even where much of it is deep and true and lasting.

No doubt the founders of the Society of Friends had their share of such instructive and at times mortifying experience.* They were brave men, and knew the reality of their own deep experience, and were not easily discouraged by a few extravagances (they appear, indeed, to have been remarkably few) amongst their followers. But there is reason to think that they were strongly impressed with the importance of specially guarding the sobriety becoming the children of the day, at a time when their own preaching was working in men's minds like new wine. Besides the one great and invariable safeguard of their constant preaching of righteousness, and appeal to the light without as the test of the reality of the light within, there were two special precautions which they consciously or unconsciously took against the danger of spiritual, or *quasi*-spiritual, excitement.

One of these was the full recognition that the action of the Spirit of God upon the heart consisted not only in impulse but in restraint, and that for its right interpretation the part of the creature was to be quiet. " Stand still in the light " is one of the familiar burdens of George Fox's advice. Friends were, and are still, as carefully taught to submit to the restraints as to yield to the impulses of " best wisdom." To " dwell deep," to " pause upon it," not to proceed unless " way opens," nor on any account to disregard a " stop in one's mind," —these and many such familiar Quaker admonitions show by how much " holy fear " their zeal has habitually been tempered.

" Quietism " is, indeed, the natural accompaniment

---

* The history of James Naylor is the best known case in point.

of "mysticism" (of mysticism, that is, in the sense of belief in the inner light). That a vivid sense of the presence of the Creator should bring stillness to the creature is inevitable. And only under the restraining and controlling power of the deep awe thus inspired can it be safe or wholesome for the human spirit to be aware of the immediate presence of its own Divine Source. There was surely a deep truth in the old Hebrew feeling, "Shall man see God and live?" Religious emotion need not be unreal to be unwholesome. The deeper the chord stirred, the more awful the danger arising from any jarring or deviation from the due and steady amount of tension.

Another precaution against the danger of yielding to excitement, or to immature or unguarded impulse is provided in our whole system of "Church government" and oversight, and especially in the importance attached to ascertaining "Friends' unity" with any proposed religious service before proceeding in it. This is a curious and beautifully adapted sheath provided for the buddings of a ministry which is free in the sense of being entirely spontaneous, prompted only by an impulse believed to be from above. It is by no means an unknown thing, perhaps not even an uncommon thing (but of this I speak from but scanty opportunities of observation), for Friends in their business meetings to discourage "concerns" which do not appear to them to be justified by reasons sufficiently weighty, or which in some other way fail to commend themselves to the judgment of the meeting.

Not only directly, but also by the indirect effect of

K

the value thus collectively and traditionally assigned to care and caution in handling spiritual things, do these recognized practices tend to inculcate sobriety and patience. And above all it is a deeply ingrained feeling in the Quaker mind that every vessel to be used for sacred purposes must before all things be clean. Everyone coming forward as a minister of the gospel especially must approve himself, or herself, in the full light of day as not only preaching, but living, according to the Spirit of Truth.

And these "ministers," be it remembered, are not people leading a sheltered and separate life : but men and women engaged in the ordinary business of life, following trades and professions, and sharing in all the daily experiences of those to whom they minister. Is there not something peculiarly adapted to the needs of our day in the combination of matter-of-fact whole-some, sober independence with the thorough-going and unreserved spirituality and purity of our acknowledged aim—that, namely, of living under the immediate guidance of the Spirit of Truth ?

It is here that I see in the ideal of Quakerism the one perennially right and fruitful ideal of Christian life—obedience to truth in the fullest and highest sense; the living truth—not truth in the sense of accurate or orthodox belief about Christ, but of an actual partaking of His Spirit, who Himself *is* the Way, the Truth, and the Life : a learning through obedience to know His voice, and a continual witness-bearing to others of the reality and the power of His living presence and teaching. We can bear this witness, in one, and only

in one, way ; our lives must be penetrated by the light
—the light which lighteth every man that cometh into
the world—penetrated and kindled and purified, till
they too shine both inwardly and outwardly. The life
is the light of men.

In our days faith is challenged at every point and at
every turn, with a freedom and a violence which was
unknown fifty years ago. All that can be shaken is
being shaken to its very foundations. My own firm
belief is that, though full of danger, this is on the whole
a natural, a necessary, and, in the main, a beneficial
process. Throw a load of fuel on a clear fire, and for
a time it may seem doubtful whether it is not
extinguished : but if the flame be strong enough, it will
rise again through the smoke and dust, and burn the
stronger for what it has mastered. And so assuredly
will faith in whatever is truly eternal rise above all
present confusions and darkenings of counsel, and burn
with fresh power in those hearts which have steadfastly cleaved to truth, be its requirements what they
may.

The Society of Friends has always refused to require
adhesion to any formularies as an express or even
implied condition of membership : and surely it has
done wisely.* It has frankly and steadily accepted

° When any person applies for membership, the Monthly Meeting appoints one or more Friends to visit the applicant, and to
report to the meeting the result of the interview, before a reply is
given. The precise conditions to be fulfilled in such cases are nowhere laid down, but the object is understood, in a general way,

the Bible as the one common standard and storehouse
of written doctrine, but it has always had the courage
to trust unreservedly to the immediate teaching of
" the Spirit which gave forth the Scriptures " for their
interpretation, and for the leading of each one " into
all truth ; " it has hitherto been true to its belief in the
living Guide.   And this, I am convinced, is the only
belief that will meet the needs of the free thought of
our day.

If thought is to be truly free, in the sense of fearless
and unbiassed, it must not only be open to the whole range
of experience, but it must be subject to the correction
of central and unchanging principles : freedom requires
stability as well as openness.   I believe that those of us
who have learned to submit to correction both from
without and from within, who dare to face at once
every real fact, and every necessary process of mental
discipline, within their reach, have a most weighty
office to fill amidst the troubled thoughts and lives of
our day.   For while human nature is what it is, it must
recognize, however dimly, that it needs not only to be
fed with knowledge, but to be strengthened with might
in the inner man.

People want, and must have if they are to be
spiritually helped at all, two things mainly at this

---

to be to ascertain that the applicant is fully " convinced of Friends'
principles."   The test is thus a purely personal and individual
one, and partakes of the elasticity which characterizes all our
arrangements, and which is felt to favour the fullest dependence
upon Divine guidance.

moment, as I believe. They want a higher, purer, worthier form of faith and worship than they have been accustomed to find provided for them ; and they want stronger proof of the reality of the objects of faith than is commonly offered.

By a higher, purer, worthier form of faith and worship, I do not mean improved formularies or liturgies ; I mean rather that openness to improvement which is precluded by fixed forms, and which the very beauty and dignity of the Anglican Liturgy tends to impede. They want, I believe, a manner of worship which shall be simpler, more living and actual—truly higher and purer because less intellectually ambitious, and more freshly inspired by human needs and Divine help ; and a manner of speaking about Divine things less conventional, less technical and artificial, arising more visibly from actual experience, and based more solidly upon common ground. They want not authorized teachers, but competent witnesses ; not to listen to sermons and religious " services," however admirable, which are delivered in fulfilment of a professional engagement, within prescribed bounds of orthodoxy, at stated times and in regular amount ; but to come into personal contact with those who have seen, felt, encountered, the things of which they speak ; and who speak not because they are officially appointed to speak, but out of the fulness of the heart because they must—people who dare be silent when they have nothing to say, and who are not afraid to acknowledge their ignorance, their doubts, or their perplexities. We are becoming critical and impatient of conventionalities, not only, as I believe, because education is spreading, but also because we are hungry for reality, because we are brought face to face (by the astonishing circulation of everything) with all manner of problems which are awful enough for us all, and doubly awful for those whose foundation is in any way insecure. In the presence—and in these days every corner of the land, not to say of the world, is in a sense present to our mental vision—in the presence of every variety of human (and animal) misery, of vice and crime and violence, and inherited degradation and disease, of changes and dangers and crumblings away of every refuge, who can wonder if men and women refuse to be satisfied with shallow or conventional explanations of the fearful problems confronting them and challenging their faith? The glibness, the exasperating completeness, the unconscious blasphemy, of many "orthodox" vindications of Providence, are enough to disgust people with mere orthodoxy.

We Christians have been roughly awakened by the storm, and are beginning to recognize that we needed such a correcting and sifting of our thought and language as modern attacks are abundantly supplying. At such a moment it is surely an unspeakable privilege for any religious body to be entirely unshackled by creeds and formularies; to have nothing in its traditions or practices to hinder it from profiting by this process of correction, or from uttering its perennial and unalterable testimony in the freshest and most flexible and modern language it can command. And perhaps it is a still greater privilege, in the midst of this Babel, to have learnt the thrice-blessed power of silence : to have secured both in private and in public the opportunity and the practice of dwelling silently upon that which is unspeakable and unchangeable : of witnessing to the light in that stillness which most clearly reflects the Divine glory, in which the accusations of the enemy are most effectually quenched.

And not only do people in these days want purer expressions of faith ; they need also stronger proofs of the reality of its objects. I do not, of course, mean new proofs ; I do not mean that really new evidence can ever be forthcoming in favour of eternal truth, though fresh aspects and illustrations and revelations of it are indeed crowding upon us day by day. I mean rather that the battle which was formerly fought by single champions here and there has now broken forth along the whole line : that in these days, whether we will or no, we are all in the thick of the fight : that no one can help hearing the deepest of all truths called in question at every turn : and that we need weapons, if not of tougher quality, yet of readier use and more thoroughly proved, more honestly our own, than those which may have sufficed in former times. We need, I believe, moral and spiritual rather than merely intellectual proof of the reality of that which alone can satisfy the human spirit in its deepest needs. Let creeds, like all other beliefs, be sifted, and tested, and corrected, and proved or disproved, and in every way dealt with as truth may require. Those whose one object is truth, can have nothing to dread from any serious and legitimate handling of any question whatever. But, when all is said and thought, it remains for ever true that man cannot by searching find out God : while yet without Him what good shall our lives do us ? It is not by supplying people with the wisest and truest replies to their difficulties that they can be effectually armed against them. Second-hand belief is poor comfort in days when authority of all kinds is so freely discredited. And at all times and under all circumstances something more than theory is required for victory.

For what, after all, is this " faith," which above all things we who have even a grain of it must desire to hold forth to others ? " This is the victory which overcometh the world, even our faith." It is a power, not a mere belief : and power can be shown only in action, only in overcoming resistance. Power that shall lift us one by one above temptations, above cares, above selfishness : power that shall make all things new, and subdue all things unto itself : power by which loss is transmuted into gain, tribulation into rejoicing, death itself into the gate of everlasting life ;—is not this the true meaning of faith ?

I see no possible means of spreading such faith as this but to exercise it ; in our own persons, as the way is prepared for us, to work righteousness, to obtain promises, out of weakness to be made strong, to wax valiant in fight—yes, and to receive our dead raised to life again. These are the proofs which will convince he world "of sin, of righteousness, and of judgment ;" these, not reasonings, are the proofs of a Divine ountain of life and power to which Friends have been taught to attach weight. Formularies, even the most perfect in their day, and the most venerable in their origin, will wear out. The meaning of language shifts, and the changing lights of knowledge distort whatever forms do not change with them ; but the power of an endless life will never lose its hold on human hearts ; and the need for help from the cloud of witnesses compassing us about was never sorer than in our own days.

Around us from all sides comes the cry, spoken or unspoken, " Give us of your oil." But we who are not unsupplied are being sternly taught to reply, " Not so ; but go ye to them that sell, and buy for yourselves."

" To them that sell." The " water of life " is for all that are athirst; the " wine and milk" are without money and without price. But the oil, the supply of light for other lives, this must truly be bought with a price. Not at second-hand, not by sitting at our ease and absorbing the thoughts of others, can we become as lamps to show forth the path of life. Our own hearts must first be baptized with fire, and our knowledge bought at the cost of suffering. It is such dearly-bought knowledge alone which can enable any one to raise a standard round which others will rally in fighting the good fight of faith.

The special struggle of our day is a struggle for truth. We who have been bold to call ourselves children of light, shall we not boldly join hands with all who are struggling towards the light? Shall we not be willing and ready to lay aside every weight,—

not only every hindering possession or habit, but every vain endeavour to bind in the truth of God by human formularies and definitions,—and unreservedly trust to the living teaching of the Spirit for ourselves and others, " looking for God *in holiness*, that we may behold His power and glory " ?

Holiness—that is, obedience—is surely the only means by which we can build, as upon the rock, a faith that will endure. Standing firmly on that rock, and on that only, we may hope to catch some glimpses of the Divine mysteries. " Clouds and darkness are round about Thee, but righteousness and truth are the habitation of Thy throne." It ill becomes us to attempt to explain all the dealings of God with man, still more the mysteries of the Divine Being and Nature; and that which must for ever remain a mystery to the most faithful of His children it is idle indeed to undertake to explain to others. Yet let us never flinch from bearing witness to that of which through these awful clouds we have from time to time been permitted to obtain some broken vision. Let us never cease to do what in us lies to persuade our fellows to lift their eyes also to the heavens, and though the vision may tarry, to wait for it in steadfast patience. They may call us dreamers, and we may think them blind. When we speak of the stars, they may say we are idly romancing about a mere painted ceiling. But the end is not yet. No roof of human workmanship will endure for ever. Sooner or later all that is of earth must perish and crumble away. Then is the time for the children of light to "lift up their heads," knowing that "their redemption draweth nigh."

For beyond all words and all proofs lies the true anchorage of the spirit, to which every firmly rooted life bears a witness neither needing or admitting of utterance. Deeper than all need of mere conviction is the need of rest and stability. We must be at rest before we can be free. In quietness and in confidence is our strength. While our hearts are tossed and agitated by every wave of this troublesome world, while the shadows of passing things have power to distract and confuse our vision, we cannot clearly discern that truth which alone can make us free.

Truly "There remaineth a rest for the people of God;" a satisfying, soul-restoring fulness of rest of which some of us have begun to taste. Some of us know assuredly that nothing perishable is the habitation of our spirits. Some of us know what it is to be willingly brought into an order flowing perceptibly and perpetually from the one unchangeable will of God, in which alone can our own will be harmonized and made steadfast. Some of us are learning ever more and more fully to accept the Father's will because it *is* the will of the Father, entering more and more truly day by day into the spirit of sonship. To experience in our own hearts the harmonizing, purifying, invigorating power of the Divine will is to be at rest for ourselves and for others; not to be set free from suffering or to become indifferent to it, but to be undisturbed by it—to know that underneath all the agitations of the creatures are the everlasting arms; to receive strength to consent to whatever is ordained by that blessed will, and to resist whatever is opposed to it.

In thus taking up the cross, we begin to see something of its glory, to experience something of its redeeming power. When we have ourselves passed from death unto life, having been led through "sundry kinds of death" into ever fuller and more abundant life, then indeed we can bear witness to the redeeming power of Christ : then we speak of what we do know, and our hands have handled, of the Word of life ; then we are on our own ground.

It has ever been our belief that the light of Christ, the brightness of the Father's glory, is (through obedience to light, even while in ignorance of its Source) purifying the hearts of many who name not His Name —who are not yet able to recognize the blessed Face from which the light shines. But the fulness of " the light which no man can approach unto " is surely reserved for those who stand before the throne of God and of the Lamb, and with full purpose of heart bow in adoration before Him that sitteth thereon.

We claim to be a people who have found rest in God ; a people building our house upon the rock, through obedience to those " words of eternal life " given forth by Christ, the Word. We recognize His Voice as speaking to us, not only in the pages of Scripture, but also in the whole course of life as ordered by Him ; and yet more closely in the inmost chamber of our own hearts ; and we desire to yield to it an undivided allegiance.

Our calling is, as branches of the living Vine, to let

the working of that Voice, Light, Spirit, and Grace of
Christ be shown forth in our own lives; and, as power
may be given us, to bear witness of it also in words;
baptizing and being baptized into the one Name in
which alone is salvation.

If, therefore, we have so unassailable a stronghold, so
deep and immovable a foundation, let us never cease
to look up steadfastly into heaven, if so be we may "see
the heavens opened;" that we may receive into our
hearts, and reflect with ever-increasing fulness in our
lives the rays of the Sun of Righteousness. The vision
may indeed be intercepted again and again by the
driving clouds: our sight may fail or falter; but the
glory itself is unchangeable, and it is in reflecting that
glory alone that any human face can be, to those that
stand by, "as the face of an angel"—of a Divinely
appointed messenger of glad tidings.

APPENDIX.

NOTE A.

THE following are the twelve queries now read, " at least once in the year," in all our meetings. The parts of the second and tenth, to which alone answers are required, are printed in italics. It should, however, be observed that " with regard to those queries to which no answer is required, Monthly Meetings are encouraged to report to their Quarterly Meetings, from time to time, on such of the subjects comprised in them as they may think desirable. Quarterly Meetings are recommended to transmit such reports, or a summary of them, to the Yearly Meeting." [*]

QUERIES.

1. What is the religious state of your meeting ? Are you individually giving evidence of true conversion of heart, and of loving devotedness to Christ ?

2. *Are your meetings for worship regularly held ; and how are they attended !* Are they occasions of

---

[*] " Book of Discipline," p. 229.

religious solemnity and edification, in which, through Christ, our ever-living High Priest and Intercessor, the Father is worshipped in spirit and in truth ?

3. Do you "walk in love, as Christ also hath loved us"? Do you cherish a forgiving spirit? Are you careful of the reputation of others ; and do you avoid and discourage tale-bearing and detraction ?

4. Are you individually frequent in reading, and diligent in meditating upon, the Holy Scriptures? And are parents and heads of households in the practice of reading them in their families in a devotional spirit, encouraging any right utterance of prayer or praise ?

5. Are you in the practice of private retirement and waiting upon the Lord ; in everything by prayer and supplication, with thanksgiving, making your requests known unto Him? And do you live in habitual dependence upon the help and guidance of the Holy Spirit ?

6. Do you maintain a religious life and conversation as becometh the gospel ? Are you watchful against conformity to the world ; against the love of ease and self-indulgence ; or being unduly absorbed by your outward concerns to the hindrance of your religious progress and your service for Christ ? And do those who have children or others under their care, endeavour by example and precept, to train them up as self-denying followers of the Lord Jesus ?

7. Do you maintain a faithful allegiance to the authority of our Lord Jesus Christ as the one Head of the Church, and the Shepherd and Bishop of souls,

from whom alone must come the true call and qualification for the ministry of the Word? And are you faithful in your testimony to the freeness of the spirituality of the gospel dispensation?

8. Are you faithful in maintaining our Christian testimony against all war, as inconsistent with the precepts and spirit of the gospel?

9. Do you maintain strict integrity in all your transactions in trade, and in your other outward concerns; and are you careful not to defraud the public revenue?

10. *Are your meetings for Church affairs regularly held; and how are they attended?* Are these meetings vigilant in the discharge of their duties towards their subordinate meetings, and in watching over the flock in the love of Christ? When delinquencies occur, are they treated timely, impartially, and in a Christian spirit? And do you individually take your right share in the attendance and service of these meetings?

11. Do you, as a Church, exercise a loving and watchful care over your younger members: promoting their instruction in fundamental Christian truth, and in the scriptural grounds of our religious principles: and manifesting an earnest desire that, through the power of Divine grace, they may all become established in the faith and hope of the gospel?

12. Do you fulfil your part as a Church, and as individuals, in promoting the cause of truth and righteousness, and the spread of the Redeemer's kingdom, at home and abroad? (1875.)

NOTE B.

HOME MISSION COMMITTEE OF THE YEARLY MEETING.

The desire felt by many Friends that the Society should, in a more systematic manner than was formerly thought necessary, recognize and provide for what is called " evangelistic " and " pastoral " work, led, in 1882, to the appointment of a Committee of the Yearly Meeting on "Home Missions." This Committee began its work by inviting the co-operation of the Monthly and Quarterly Meetings, and in its first Annual Report it mentions that ten of the Quarterly Meetings had appointed Committees to correspond with it; in the next year thirteen of the Quarterly Meetings were thus in correspondence with the Home Mission Committee; and in 1887 the Report states that the Home Mission Committee itself includes members of every Quarterly Meeting except one.

In 1888, the number of Friends working in connection with the Home Mission Committee was nineteen. The Report of 1889 speaks of a considerable extension of the work of the Committee, but does not give the number of workers.

The donations and subscriptions received by the Committee in the year ending May, 1889, amounted to £2,333.

The work undertaken by " Home Mission Friends " is of various kinds; such as conducting first day schools, Bible classes, temperance meetings, lecturing on Friends' principles, in some neighbourhoods visiting the sick and the poor, and in various ways endeavouring to build up and strengthen meetings which seem to be in need of help.

Notwithstanding the large measure of support which the Committee has met with, there are many Friends who feel very serious hesitation about this practice of providing " pastoral care," and who fear lest it should tend to weaken, if not to destroy, the force of our testimony against a paid or humanly appointed ministry. The danger is obvious ; and I shall not attempt to estimate the degree in which it can be averted, or the force of the reasons for encountering it. I will content myself with making from the Reports of the Committee a few extracts bearing upon this question.

" We have been forcibly impressed with the extent and variety of openings for service which have presented themselves to us. Much of this work is of a character which can, we believe, be more effectually performed by the Society of Friends than by any other religious body. . . . In two instances we have deemed it right to give pecuniary assistance to Friends who felt it laid upon them, as a religious duty, to give the whole or a greater part of their time to the work. . . . These arrangements involve no bargain or understanding whatsoever for the preaching of the gospel, and their work has been largely of an organizing character." (1883).

" It is found that Friends in all parts of the country are watchful lest a separate class of supported ministers should be set up, and this is a matter which has from the first received our very serious attention. It is our practice, when a Friend has offered his services to this Committee, not to enter upon the question of the amount or manner of support to be granted him until after he has been accepted by us. We have carefully avoided the establishment of any scale of maintenance, each case being separately considered on the basis of the actual needs and circumstances of the Friend in question ; and we have encouraged Friends, where practicable, to contribute by their labour to their own support." (1886.)

" We are glad to report an increase in the number of those who require no pecuniary assistance beyond necessary expenses when actually on religious service. About half the workers are living on their private means, or partially maintaining themselves by their labour. About half of the number may also be considered as stationed more or less in one place, and the remainder as engaged in evangelistic visits to various towns as way may open. Of the resident workers, several have travelled with minutes from their Monthly Meetings, or have rendered temporary assistance to particular meetings by request of other Monthly Meetings than their own. . . . In the meetings where our workers are resident, the voices of many new members are frequently heard in exhortation and prayer. In one of them a visiting Friend desired a meeting with all those who took vocal part in meetings. No fewer than thirteen responed to his invitation, while three or four more were prevented by other engagements. . . . We believe our workers are, without exception, loyal to the testimony of the Society against the establishment, directly or indirectly, of a ' one-man ministry.' . . . Since the formation of this Committee there is hardly a Quarterly Meeting in which they " (the Friends engaged in " evangelistic " work) " have not travelled, in several of them many times and for many weeks together. . . . Some of these visits have originated in concerns of the Friends themselves. In other cases the way has been made for them by an invitation of a Quarterly, Monthly, or particular Meeting, or the Committee of some Friends' mission or adult school. In no case has this Committee deemed it consistent to SEND any worker anywhere, or to do more than lay such invitation before him, leaving it to his own conviction of duty as to whether he can see his way to accept it or not." (1888.)

" With one exception, every Friend in connection with us has been engaged during the year to a greater or less extent in work outside the meeting in which he resides." (1889.)

NOTE C.

SLAVERY.

In the introduction by J. G. Whittier to a recent edition of John Woodman's " Journal,"[°] there is a remarkable account of the manner in which our Society in America was gradually freed from all complicity with slavery,

---

[°] Published by Robert Smeal, Glasgow. 1883.

long before the struggle for its abolition was begun elsewhere; from which I venture to make some extracts, for the sake of the illustration it affords of the working both of our principles and of our machinery.

From the time of George Fox himself, who in 1671 visited Barbados, and admonished those who held slaves there to bear in mind that they were brethren, and that "after certain years of servitude they should make them free," voices had been raised again and again in several of the American meetings to witness against the buying and keeping of slaves.

In 1742, John Woolman, then in the employment of a small storekeeper in New Jersey, was desired by his master to make out a bill of sale of a negro slave-woman. "On taking up his pen," says Whittier, "the young clerk felt a sudden and strong scruple in his mind. The thought of writing an instrument of slavery for one of his fellow-creatures oppressed him. God's voice against the desecration of His image spoke in his soul. He yielded to the will of his employer, but while writing the instrument he was constrained to declare, both to the buyer and the seller, that he believed slave-keeping inconsistent with the Christian religion." This circumstance "was the starting-point of a life-long testimony against slavery.

"In the year 1746, he visited Maryland, Virginia, and North Carolina. He was afflicted by the prevalence of slavery. It appeared to him, in his own words, 'as a dark gloominess overhanging the land.' On his return, he wrote an essay on the subject, which was

published in 1754. Three years after, he made a second
visit to the Southern meetings of Friends. Travelling
as a minister of the gospel, he was compelled to sit
down at the tables of slave-holding planters, who
were accustomed to entertain their friends free of cost,
and who could not comprehend the scruples of their
guest against receiving as a gift food and lodging which
he regarded as the gains of oppression. He was a poor
man, but he loved truth more than money. He
therefore placed the pay for his entertainment in the
hands of some member of the family, for the benefit of
the slaves, or gave it directly to them as he had
opportunity. . . .

"The annual assemblage of the Yearly Meeting in
1758 at Philadelphia* must ever be regarded as one of
the most important religious convocations in the history
of the Christian Church. The labours of Woolman and
his few but earnest associates had not been in vain. A
deep and tender interest had been awakened, and this
meeting was looked forward to with varied feelings of
solicitude by all parties. All felt that the time had
come for some definite action. . . . . At length,"
after a "solemn and weighty appeal" from John
Woolman, "the truth in a great measure triumphed

° It must be remembered that the Society of Friends in
America consists of many Yearly Meetings, each of which is
supreme and independent within its own compass. Their number
has considerably increased since John Woolman's time ; and in
the Western States there is also a rapid increase in the number of
members.

over opposition ; and, without any public dissent, the meeting agreed that the injunction of our Lord and Saviour, to do to others as we would that others should do to us, should induce Friends who held slaves 'to set them at liberty, making a Christian provision for them ; ' and four Friends " (of whom John Woolman was one) " were approved of as suitable persons to visit and treat with such as kept slaves, within the limits of the meeting.

" This painful and difficult duty was faithfully performed. . . . These labours were attended with the blessing of the God of the poor and oppressed. Dealing in slaves was almost entirely abandoned, and many who held slaves set them at liberty. But many members still continuing the practice, a more emphatic testimony against it was issued by the Yearly Meeting in 1774 ; and two years after, the subordinate meetings were directed to deny the right of membership to such as persisted in holding their fellow-men as property. . . . In the year 1760, John Woolman, in the course of a religious visit to New England," attended their Yearly Meeting, where " the London Epistle for 1758, condemning the unrighteous traffic in men, was read, and the substance of it embodied in the discipline of the meeting ; and the following query was adopted, to be answered by the subordinate meetings : ' Are Friends clear of importing negroes, or buying them when imported ; and do they use those well where they are possessed by inheritance or otherwise, endeavouring to train them up in principles of religion ?' . . . In 1769, at the suggestion of the Rhode Island

Quarterly Meeting, the Yearly Meeting expressed its sense of the wrongfulness of holding slaves, and appointed a large committee to visit those members who were implicated in the practice. . . . It was stated, in the epistle to London Yearly Meeting of the year 1772, that a few Friends had freed their slaves from bondage, but that others ' have been so reluctant thereto, that they *have been disowned** for not complying with the advice of this meeting.'

" In 1773, the following minute was made : ' It is our sense that truth not only requires the young of capacity and ability, but likewise the aged and impotent, and also all in a state of infancy and nonage, among Friends, to be discharged and set free from a state of slavery ; that we do no more claim property in the human race, as we do in the beasts that perish.'

" In 1782, no slaves were known to be held in the New England Yearly Meeting. The next year, it was recommended to the subordinate meetings to appoint Committees to effect a proper and just *settlement between the manumitted slaves and their former masters for their past services.* In 1784, it was concluded by the Yearly Meeting that any slaveholder who refused to comply with the award of these committees should, after due care and labour with him, be disowned from the Society. This was effectual ; settlements without disownment were made to the satisfaction of all parties, and every case was disposed of previous to the year 1787.

---

* The Italics are throughout Whittier's.

" In the New York Yearly Meeting, slave-trading was prohibited about the middle of the last century. In 1771, in consequence of an epistle from the Philadelphia Yearly Meeting, a committee was appointed to visit those who held slaves, and to advise with them in relation to emancipation. In 1776, it was made a disciplinary offence to buy, sell, or hold slaves upon any condition. In 1784, but one slave was to be found in the limits of the meeting. In the same year, by answers from the several subordinate meetings, it was ascertained that an equitable settlement for past services had been effected between the emancipated negroes and their masters in all but three cases.

" In the Virginia Yearly Meeting slavery had its strongest hold." In 1757, it condemned the foreign slave trade. In 1764, it enjoined upon its members the duty of kindness towards their servants, of educating them, and carefully providing for their food and clothing. Four years after, its members were strictly prohibited from purchasing any more slaves. In 1773, it earnestly recommended the immediate manumission of all slaves held in bondage, after the females had reached eighteen and the males twenty-one years of age. At the same time it was advised that committees should be appointed for the purpose of instructing the emancipated persons in the principles of morality and of religion, and for advising and aiding them in their temporal concerns. . . .

" In 1784, the different Quarterly Meetings having reported that many still held slaves, notwithstanding the advice and entreaties of their friends, the Yearly

Meeting directed that, where *endeavours* to convince those offenders of their error proved ineffectual, the Monthly Meeting should proceed to disown them. We have no means of ascertaining the precise number of those actually disowned for slave-holding in the Virginia Yearly Meeting, but it is well known to have been very small. In almost all cases the care and assiduous labours of those who had the welfare of the Society and of humanity at heart were successful in inducing offenders to manumit their slaves, and confess their error in resisting the wishes of their friends, and bringing reproach upon the cause of truth.

"So ended slavery in the Society of Friends. For three-quarters of a century the advice put forth in the meetings of the Society at stated intervals, that Friends should be ' careful to maintain their testimony against slavery,' has been adhered to, so far as owning, or even hiring a slave is concerned. Apart from its firstfruits of emancipation, there is a perennial value in the example exhibited of the power of truth, urged patiently and in earnest love, to overcome the difficulties in the way of the eradication of an evil system, strengthened by long habit, entangled with all the complex relations of Society, and closely allied with the love of power, the pride of family, and the lust of gain."

I need hardly remind my readers of the singular interest of John Woolman's own account of his experiences in this and other matters, which would scarcely admit of abridgment. I have, therefore, been obliged, though unwillingly, to content myself with the above bare enumeration of the actual steps taken by the

various meetings, without making any attempt to show
to what an extent John Woolman's own deep exercises of
mind contributed to bring them about.   For a study of
Quaker experience, in its purest and most impressive
form, the " Journal " itself is perhaps unrivalled.

NOTE D.

The meetings for worship now held in London are as
follows :—

1. DEVONSHIRE HOUSE (12, Bishopsgate Street
   Without).
   Sunday, 11 a.m. and 6.30 p.m.
   Tuesday, 10.30 a.m. (omitted in Q. M. week).
   Wednesday, 6.30 p.m.

2. PEEL (Peel Court, John Street, Smithfield).
   Sunday, 11 a.m. and 6.30 p.m.
   Wednesday, 10 a.m.

3. STOKE NEWINGTON (Park Street, Church Street).
   Sunday, 10.30 a.m. and 6 p.m.
   Thursday, 10.30 a.m.

4. WANDSWORTH (High Street).
   Sunday, 11 a.m. and 4.30 p.m.
   Thursday, 7 p.m. (omitted in M. M. and Q. M.
   weeks).

5. HAMMERSMITH (Waterloo).
   Sunday, 11 a.m. and 6.30 p.m.

6. UPPER HOLLOWAY (Mercer's Road).
    Sunday, 10 a.m., 11 a.m., and 6.30 p.m.
    Wednesday, 10.30 a.m. (omitted in Y. M., Q. M.,
        and M. M. weeks).

7. WESTMINSTER (52, St. Martin's Lane, Charing
        Cross).
    Sunday, 11 a.m. and 6.30 p.m.
    Thursday, 10 a.m. (omitted in Q.M. and M.M.
        weeks).

There are sixteen other meetings for worship belonging to London and Middlesex Quarterly Meeting; but as they are suburban rather than metropolitan, I do not include them in this list.

Meetings for worship are also (by permission of the Monthly Meeting) appointed to be held for the present at

    CHELSEA (48, Cheyne Walk).
    Sunday, 4 p.m.
    Tuesday, 4 p.m.

All particulars respecting meetings all over the country are to be found in a small sixpenny volume, called the "Friends' Book of Meetings," published annually (by direction of the Yearly Meeting) by E. Hicks, Jun., 14, Bishopsgate Street Without, E.C.

THE END.